W9-BTE-400

TALES of DEATH and DEMENTIA

"Quoth the Raven, "NEVERMORE."

Atheneum Books for Young Readers

An imprint of Simon & Schuster Children's Publishing Division

1230 Avenue of the Americas, New York, New York 10020

Text abridgment copyright © 2009 by Simon & Schuster, Inc.

Illustrations copyright © 2009 by Gris Grimly

Book design by Michael McCartney

The text of this book is set in Locarno.

The illustrations are rendered in pen, ink, and watercolor.

Manufactured in the United States of America

First edition

10 9 8 7 6 5 4 3 2 1

Library of Congress Cataloging-in-Publication Data

Poe, Edgar Allan, 1809—1849.

Edgar Allan Poe's tales of death and dementia / Edgar Allan Poe ; illustrated by Gris Grimly.—1st ed.

p. cm.

Summary: Four short stories, abridged and illustrated, by the nineteenth-century American writer best known for his tales of horror.

ISBN 978-1-4169-5025-7

1: Horror tales, American. 2. Children's stories, American. [1. Horror stories. 2. Short stories.] I. Grimly, Gris, ill. II. Title. III. Title: Tales of death and dementia.

PZ7.P7515Ef 2009

[Fic]—dc22 2009003056

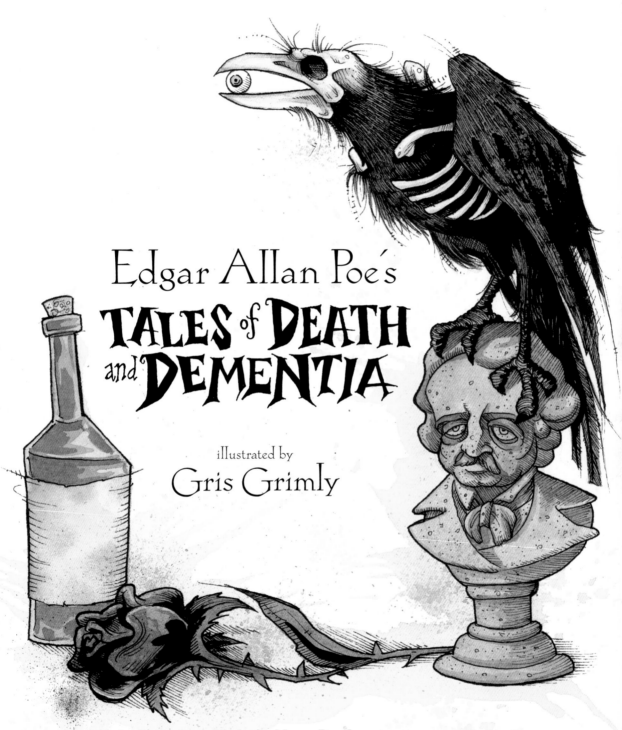

Edgar Allan Poe's
TALES of DEATH
and DEMENTIA

illustrated by
Gris Grimly

Atheneum Books for Young Readers
New York London Toronto Sydney

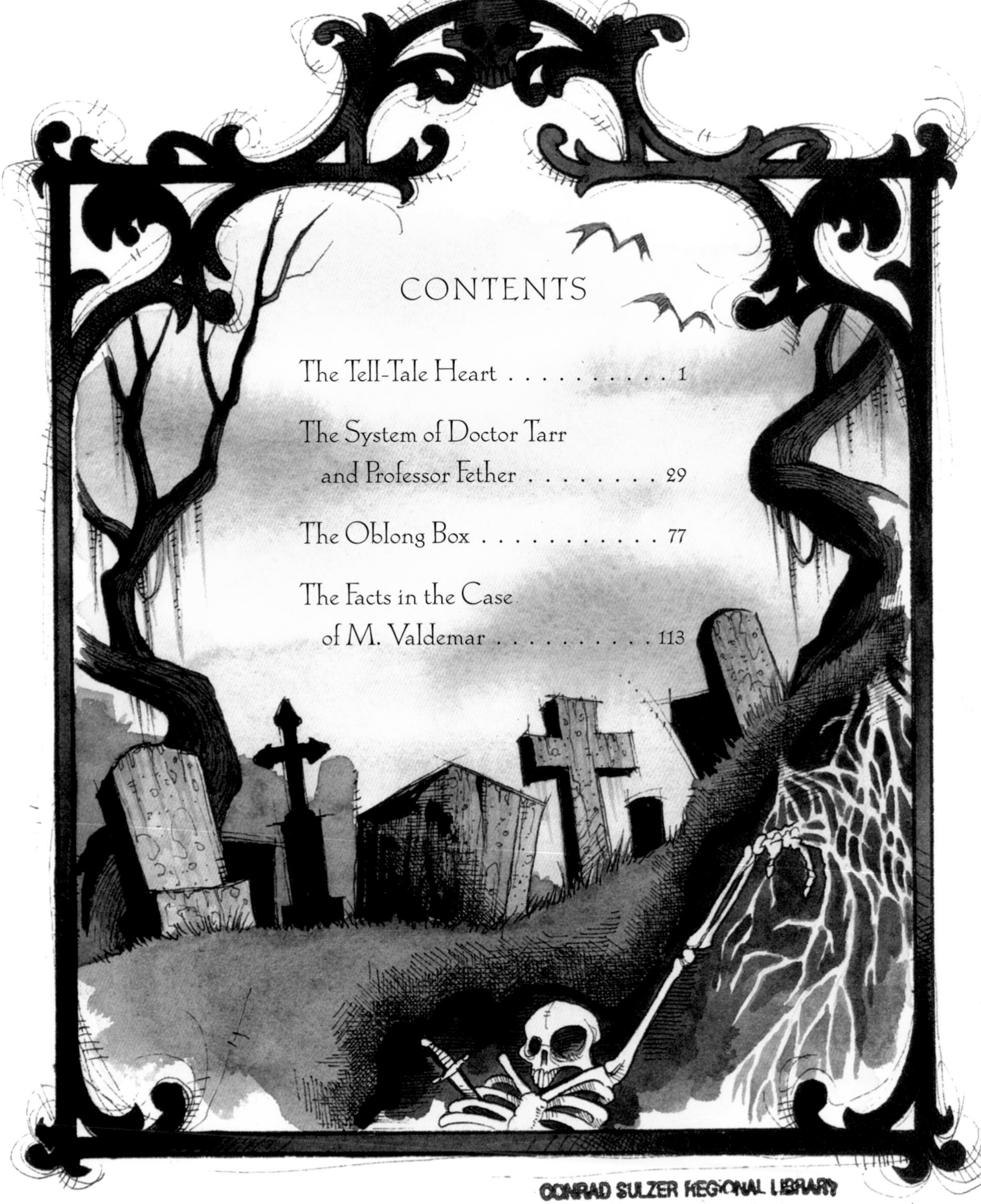

CONTENTS

The Tell-Tale Heart

True! — nervous — very, very dreadfully nervous I had been and am, but why will you say that I am mad?

The disease had sharpened my senses — not destroyed, not dulled them. Above all was the sense of hearing acute. I heard all things in the heaven and in the earth. I heard many things in hell. How, then, am I mad?

Hearken! and observe how healthily, how calmly I can tell you the whole story.

It is impossible to say how first the idea entered my brain, but, once conceived, it haunted me day and night. Object there was none. Passion there was none. I loved the old man. He had never wronged me. He had never given me insult. For his gold I had no desire.

I think it was his eye!

THE OLD MAN

Yes, it was this! He had the eye of a vulture — a pale blue eye, with a film over it.

Whenever it fell upon me, my blood ran cold; and so by degrees — very gradually — I made up my mind to take the life of the old man, and thus rid myself of the eye forever.

Now this is the point, you fancy me mad. Madmen know nothing. But you should have seen me. You should have seen how wisely I proceeded — with what caution — with what foresight — with what dissimulation I went to work!

I was never kinder to the old man than during the whole week before I killed him. And every night, about midnight, I turned the latch of his door and opened it — oh so gently! And then, when I had made an opening sufficient for my head, I put in a dark lantern, all closed — closed, that no light shone out — and then I thrust in my head.

Oh, you would have laughed to see how cunningly I thrust it in! I moved it slowly — very, very slowly, so that I might not disturb the old man's sleep. It took me an hour to place my whole head within the opening so far that I could see him as he lay upon his bed.

Ha! Would a madman have been so wise as this?

And then, when my head was well in the room, I undid the lantern cautiously — oh so cautiously — cautiously (for the hinges creaked) — I undid it just so much that a single thin ray fell upon the vulture eye.

And this I did for seven long nights — every night just at midnight. But I found the eye always closed; and so it was impossible to do the work, for it was not the old man who vexed me, but his Evil Eye.

And every morning, when the day broke, I went boldly into the chamber, and spoke courageously to him, calling him by name in a hearty tone, and inquiring how he had passed the night. So, you see, he would have been a very profound old man, indeed, to suspect that every night, just at twelve, I looked in upon him while he slept.

Upon the eighth night I was more than usually cautious in opening the door. A watch's minute hand moves more quickly than did mine. Never before that night had I felt the extent of my own powers, of my sagacity.

I could scarcely contain my feelings of triumph. To think that there I was, opening the door, little by little, and he not even to dream of my secret deeds or thoughts. I fairly chuckled at the idea; and perhaps he heard me, for he moved on the bed suddenly, as if startled. Now, you may think that I drew back — but no. His room was as black as pitch with the thick darkness (for the shutters were close fastened, through fear of robbers), and so I knew that he could not see the opening of the door, and I kept pushing it on steadily, steadily.

I had my head in, and was about to open the lantern when my thumb slipped upon the tin fastening, and the old man sprang up in the bed, crying out —

"Who's there?"

I kept quite still and said nothing.

For a whole hour I did not move a muscle, and in the meantime I did not hear him lie down. He was still sitting up in the bed, listening — just as I have done, night after night, hearkening to the death watches in the wall.

Presently I heard a slight groan, and I knew
it was the groan of mortal terror. It was not a
groan of pain or of grief — oh, no! It was the
low stifled sound that arises from the bottom of
the soul when overcharged with awe.
I knew the sound well. Many a night, just
at midnight, when all the world slept, it has
welled up from my own bosom, deepening, with
its dreadful echo, the terrors that distracted
me. I say I knew it well. I knew what the old
man felt, and pitied him, although I chuckled
at heart. I knew that he had been lying awake
ever since the first slight noise, when he had
turned in the bed. His fears had been ever
since growing upon him. He had been trying
to fancy them causeless, but could not.

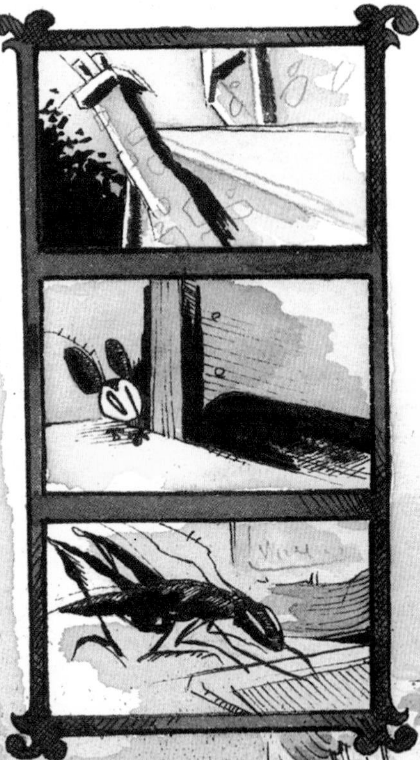

He had been saying to himself, "It is nothing but the wind in the chimney — it is only a mouse crossing the floor" or "It is merely a cricket which has made a single chirp." Yes, he has been trying to comfort himself with these suppositions, but he had found all in vain. All in vain because Death, in approaching him, had stalked with his black shadow before him, and enveloped the victim.

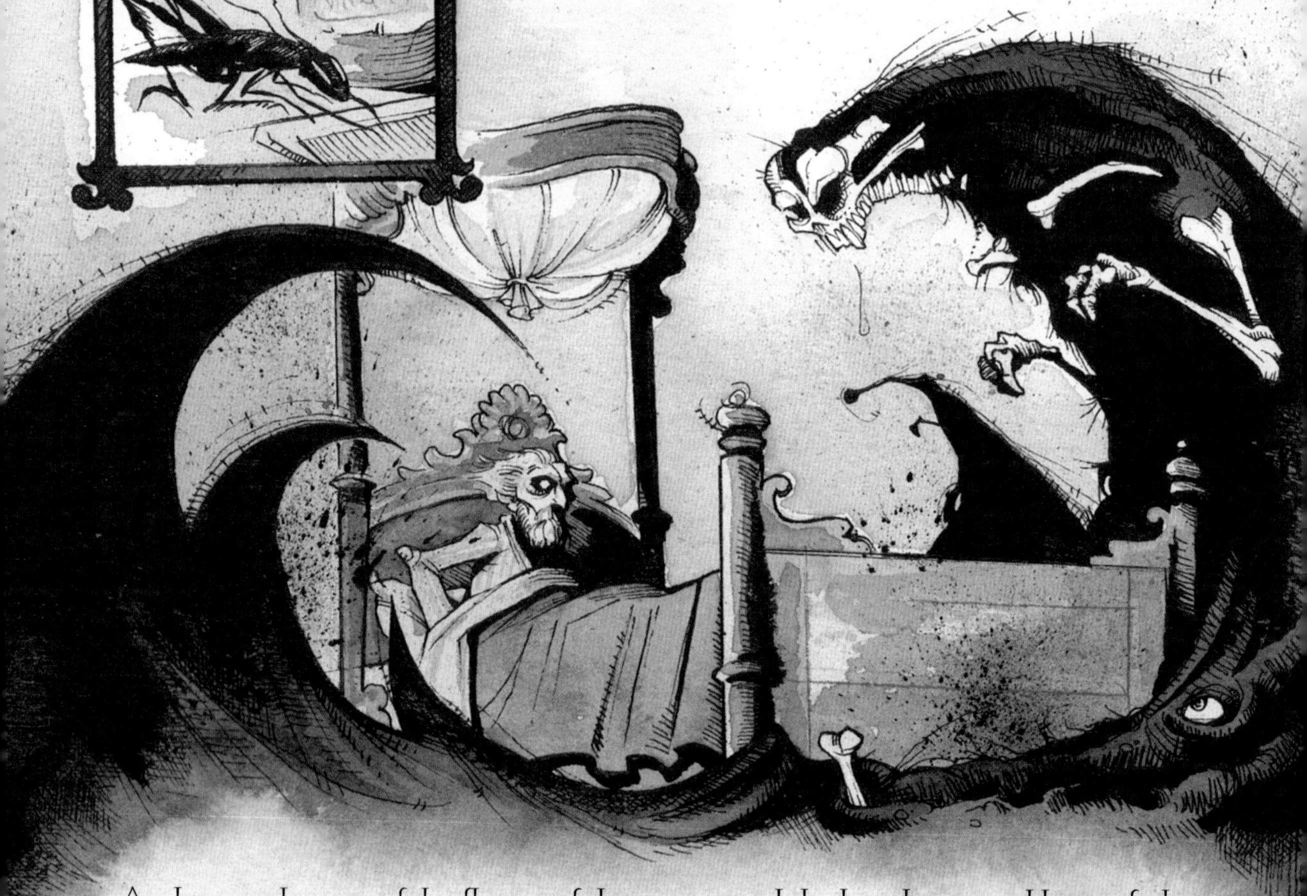

And it was the mournful influence of the unperceived shadow that caused him to feel — although he neither saw nor heard — to feel the presence of my head within the room.

When I had waited a long time,
very patiently, without hearing him
lie down, I resolved to open a little — a very,
very little crevice in the lantern. So I opened it — you
cannot imagine how stealthily, stealthily — until, at length, a
simple dim ray, like the thread of the spider, shot from
out the crevice and fell upon the vulture eye.

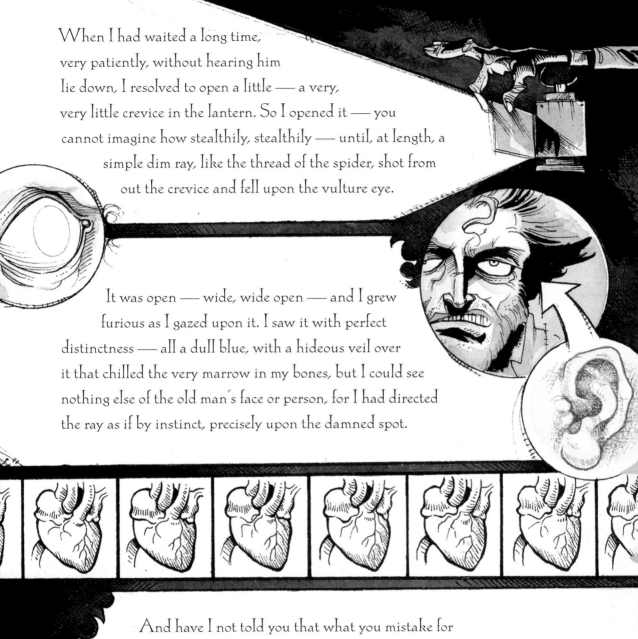

It was open — wide, wide open — and I grew
furious as I gazed upon it. I saw it with perfect
distinctness — all a dull blue, with a hideous veil over
it that chilled the very marrow in my bones, but I could see
nothing else of the old man's face or person, for I had directed
the ray as if by instinct, precisely upon the damned spot.

And have I not told you that what you mistake for
madness is but overacuteness of the senses? Now, I say,
there came to my ears a low, dull, quick sound, such as a
watch makes when enveloped in cotton. I knew that sound well,
too. It was the beating of the old man's heart. It increased my fury,
as the beating of a drum stimulates the soldier into courage.

11

But even yet I refrained and kept still. I scarcely breathed. I held the lantern motionless. I tried how steadily I could maintain the ray upon the eye.

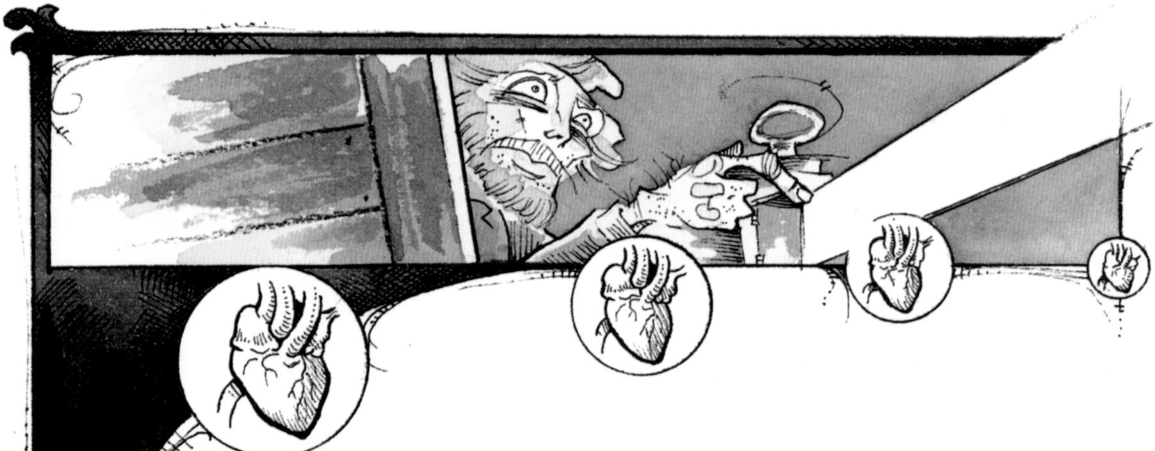

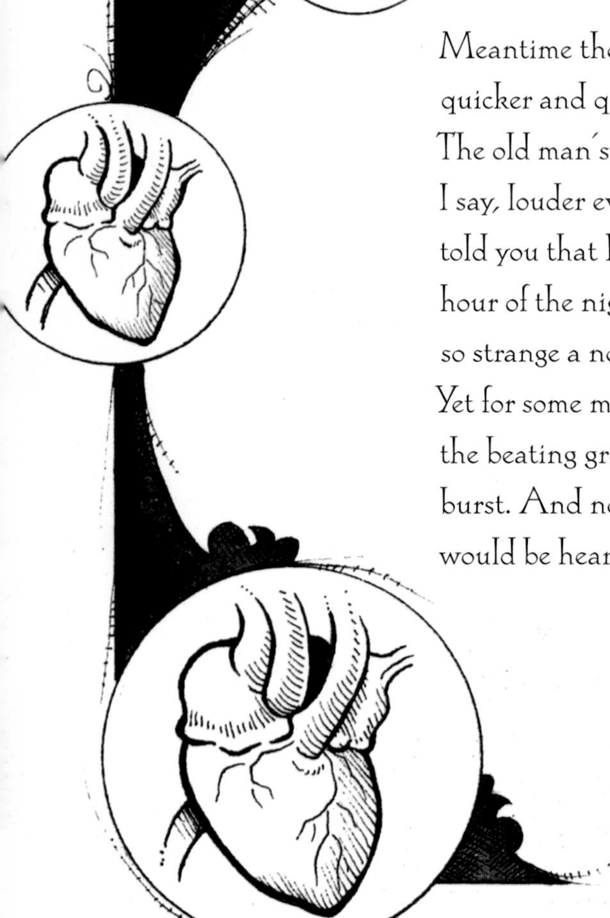

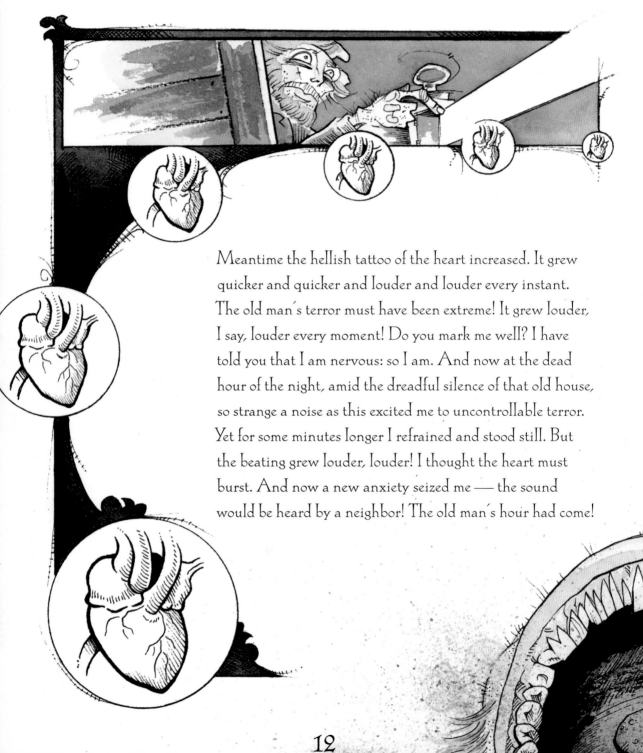

Meantime the hellish tattoo of the heart increased. It grew quicker and quicker and louder and louder every instant. The old man's terror must have been extreme! It grew louder, I say, louder every moment! Do you mark me well? I have told you that I am nervous: so I am. And now at the dead hour of the night, amid the dreadful silence of that old house, so strange a noise as this excited me to uncontrollable terror. Yet for some minutes longer I refrained and stood still. But the beating grew louder, louder! I thought the heart must burst. And now a new anxiety seized me — the sound would be heard by a neighbor! The old man's hour had come!

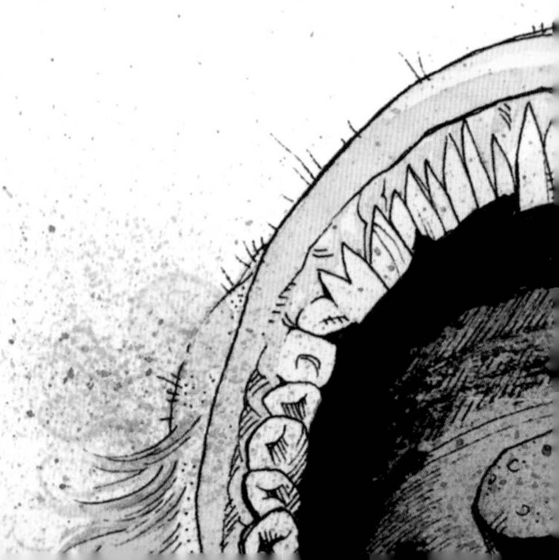

With a loud yell, I threw open the lantern and leaped into the room. He shrieked once — once only.

In an instant I dragged him to the floor and pulled the heavy bed over him.

13

I then smiled gaily to find the deed so far done. But for many minutes the heart beat on with a muffled sound. This, however, did not vex me; it would not be heard through the wall. At length it ceased. The old man was dead.

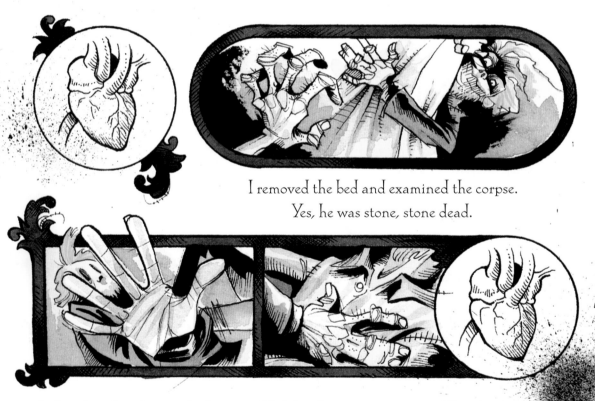

I removed the bed and examined the corpse.
Yes, he was stone, stone dead.

I placed my hand upon the heart and held it there many minutes. There was no pulsation. He was stone dead. His eye would trouble me no more.

If still you think me mad, you will think so no longer when I describe the wise precautions I took for the concealment of the body. The night waned, and I worked hastily but in silence.

I then took up three planks from the flooring of the chamber, and deposited all between the scantlings. I then replaced the boards so cleverly, so cunningly that no human eye — not even his — could have detected anything wrong. There was nothing to wash out — no stain of any kind — no blood spot whatever. I had been too wary for that.

When I had made an end of these labors, it was four
o'clock — still dark as midnight. As the bell sounded
the hour, there came a knocking at the street door.
I went down to open it with a light heart,
for what had I now to fear?

There entered three men, who introduced themselves, with perfect suavity, as
officers of the police. A shriek had been heard by a neighbor during the night;
suspicion of foul play had been aroused; information had been lodged at the
police office, and they (the officers) had been deputed to search the premises.

I smiled, for what had I to fear? I bade the gentlemen welcome. The shriek, I said, was my own in a dream. The old man, I mentioned, was absent in the country.

I took my visitors all over the house. I bade them search — search well. I led them, at length, to his chamber. I showed them his treasures, secure, undisturbed.

In the enthusiasm of my confidence, I brought chairs into the room, and desired them here to rest from their fatigues while I myself, in the wild audacity of my perfect triumph, placed my own seat upon the very spot beneath which reposed the corpse of the victim.

The officers were satisfied. My manner had convinced them. I was singularly at ease. They sat, and while I answered cheerily, they chatted of familiar things. But ere long, I felt myself getting pale, and wished them gone. My head ached, and I fancied a ringing in my ears, but still they sat, and still chatted. The ringing became more distinct.

I talked more freely to get rid of the feeling, but it continued and gained definiteness — until, at length, I found that the noise was not within my ears.

No doubt I now grew very pale, but I talked more fluently and with a heightened voice. Yet the sound increased — and what could I do? It was a low, dull, quick sound — much such a sound as a watch makes when enveloped in cotton. I gasped for breath — and yet the officers heard it not. I talked more quickly — more vehemently — but the noise steadily increased. I arose and argued about trifles, in a high key and with violent gesticulations, but the noise steadily increased.

Why would they not be gone?

I paced the floor to and fro with heavy strides, as if excited to fury by the observations of the men, but the noise steadily increased. Oh God! What could I do?

21

I foamed — I raved — I swore!

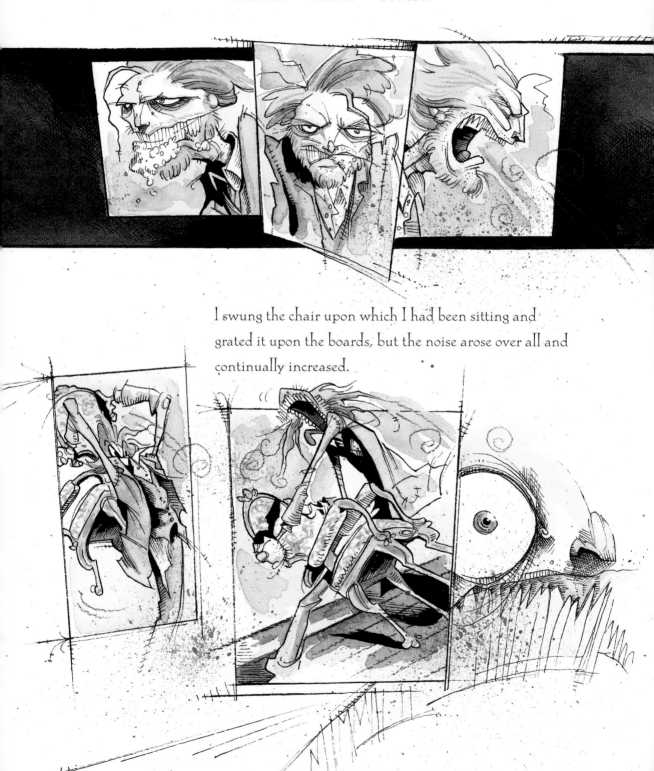

I swung the chair upon which I had been sitting and grated it upon the boards, but the noise arose over all and continually increased.

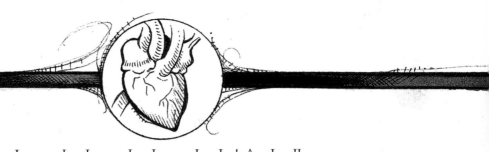

It grew louder — louder — louder! And still
the men chatted pleasantly, and smiled.

Was it possible they heard not? Almighty God! — No, no!
They heard! — They suspected! — They knew! — They
were making a mockery of my horror! This I thought, and this I
think. But anything was better than this agony! Anything was
more tolerable than this derision! I could bear those hypocritical
smiles no longer! I felt that I must scream or die! — And
now — Again! — Hark! Louder! Louder! Louder! Louder! —

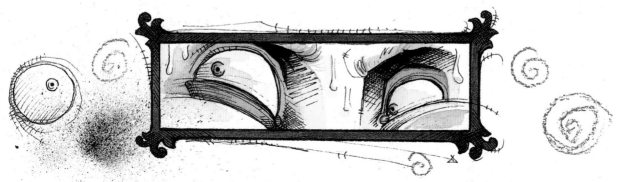

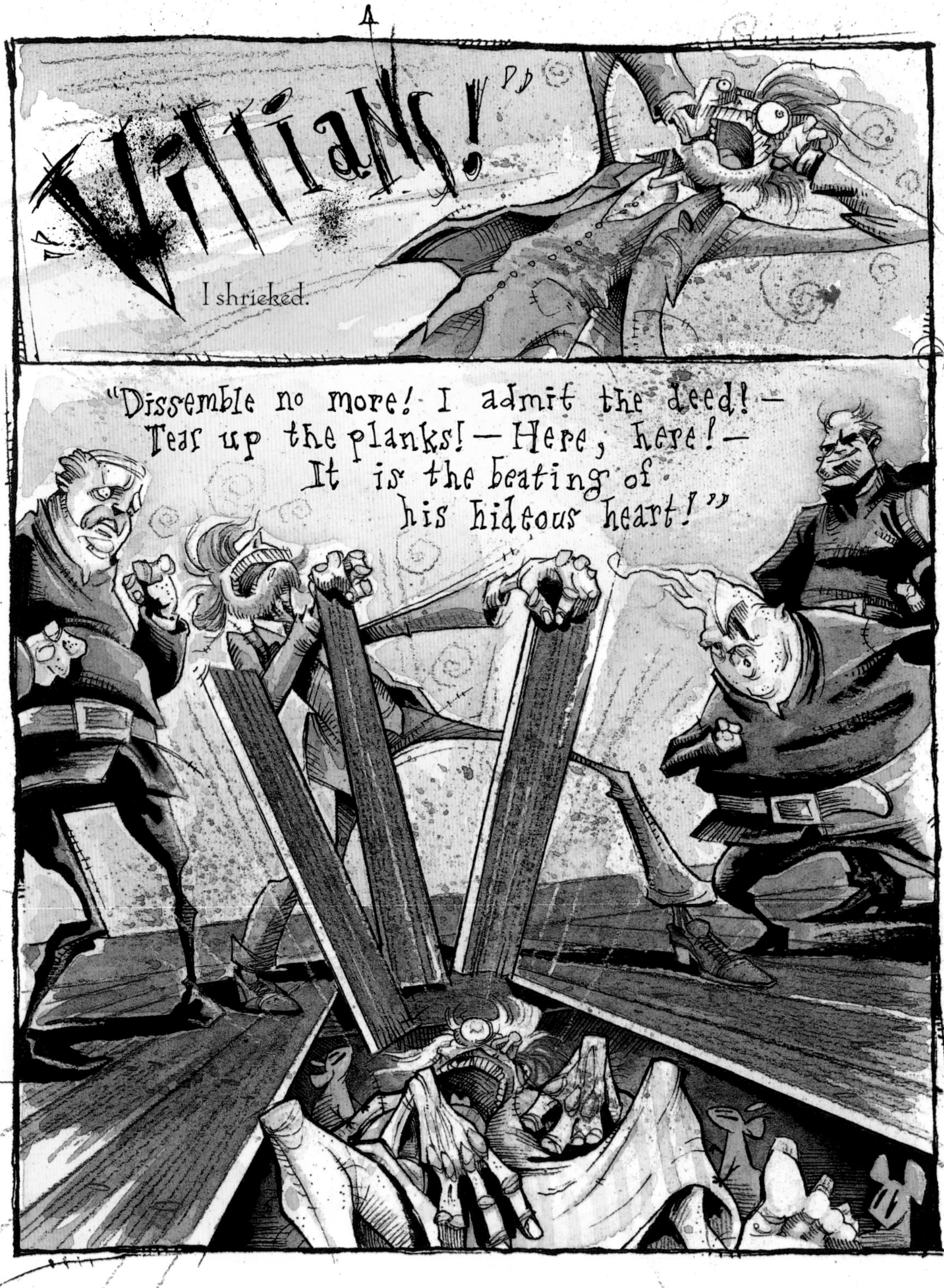
"Villians!"
I shrieked.
"Dissemble no more! I admit the deed!—
Tear up the planks!—Here, here!—
It is the beating of
his hideous heart!"

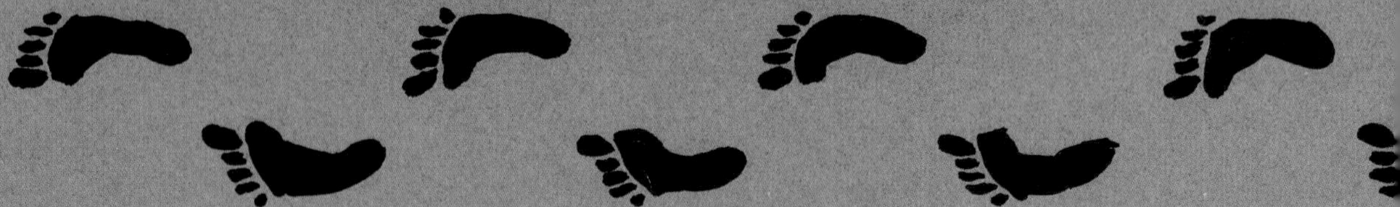

The System of Doctor Tarr and Professor Fether

While on a tour through Southern France, my route led me within a few miles of a certain Maison de Santé or private madhouse, about which I had heard much, in Paris, from my medical friends.

As I had never visited a place of the kind, I proposed to my traveling companion that we should turn aside, and look through the establishment. To this he objected — pleading a very usual horror at the sight of a lunatic. He begged me, however, not to let any mere courtesy toward himself interfere with the gratification of my curiosity.

As he bade me good-bye, I bethought me that there might be some difficulty in obtaining access to the premises, and mentioned my fears on this point. He replied that, in fact, unless I had personal knowledge of the superintendent, Monsieur Maillard, or some credential in the way of a letter, a difficulty might be found to exist. For himself, he added, he had, some years since, made the acquaintance of Maillard, and would so far assist me as to ride up to the door and introduce me, although his feelings on the subject of lunacy would not permit his entering the house.

We entered a grass-grown by-path, which, in half an hour, nearly lost itself in a dense forest, clothing the base of a mountain.

Through this dank and gloomy wood we rode some two miles, when the Maison de Santé came in view. It was a fantastic château, much dilapidated, and, indeed, scarcely tenantable through age and neglect. Its aspect inspired me with absolute dread, and, checking my horse, I half resolved to turn back. I soon, however, grew ashamed of my weakness, and proceeded.

As we rode up to the gateway, I perceived it slightly open, and the visage of a man peering through.

This man came forth, accosted my companion by name, shook him cordially by the hand, and begged him to alight. It was Monsieur Maillard himself.

He was a portly, fine-looking gentleman with a certain air of gravity, dignity, and authority, which was very impressive.

My friend, having presented me, mentioned my desire to inspect the establishment, and received Monsieur Maillard's assurance that he would show me all attention, now took leave, and I saw him no more.

The superintendent ushered me into a small and exceedingly neat parlor, containing, among other indications of refined taste, many books, drawings, pots of flowers, and musical instruments. A cheerful fire blazed upon the hearth.

At a piano, singing an aria from Bellini, sat a young and very beautiful woman, who, at my entrance, paused in her song, and received me with graceful courtesy. Her voice was low, and her whole manner subdued. I thought, too, that I perceived the traces of sorrow in her countenance, which was excessively, although to my taste, not unpleasingly pale.

I had heard that the institution of Monsieur Maillard was managed upon what is vulgarly termed the "system of soothing" — that all punishments were avoided — that even confinement was seldom resorted to — that the patients, while secretly watched, were left much apparent liberty, and that most of them were permitted to roam about the house and grounds in the ordinary apparel of persons in right mind.

Keeping these impressions in view, I was cautious in what I said before the young lady, for I could not be sure that she was sane; and, in fact, there was a certain restless brilliancy about her eyes which half led me to imagine she was not.

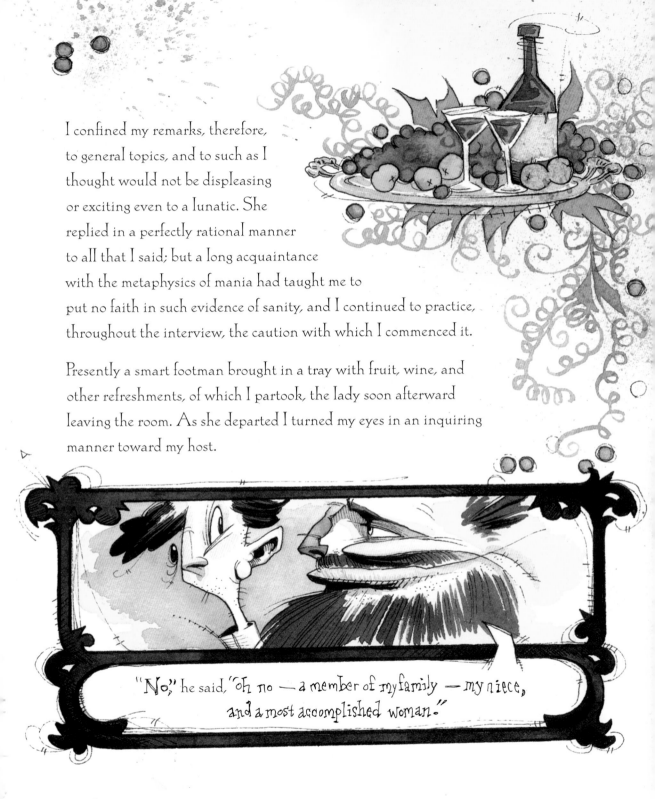

I confined my remarks, therefore, to general topics, and to such as I thought would not be displeasing or exciting even to a lunatic. She replied in a perfectly rational manner to all that I said; but a long acquaintance with the metaphysics of mania had taught me to put no faith in such evidence of sanity, and I continued to practice, throughout the interview, the caution with which I commenced it.

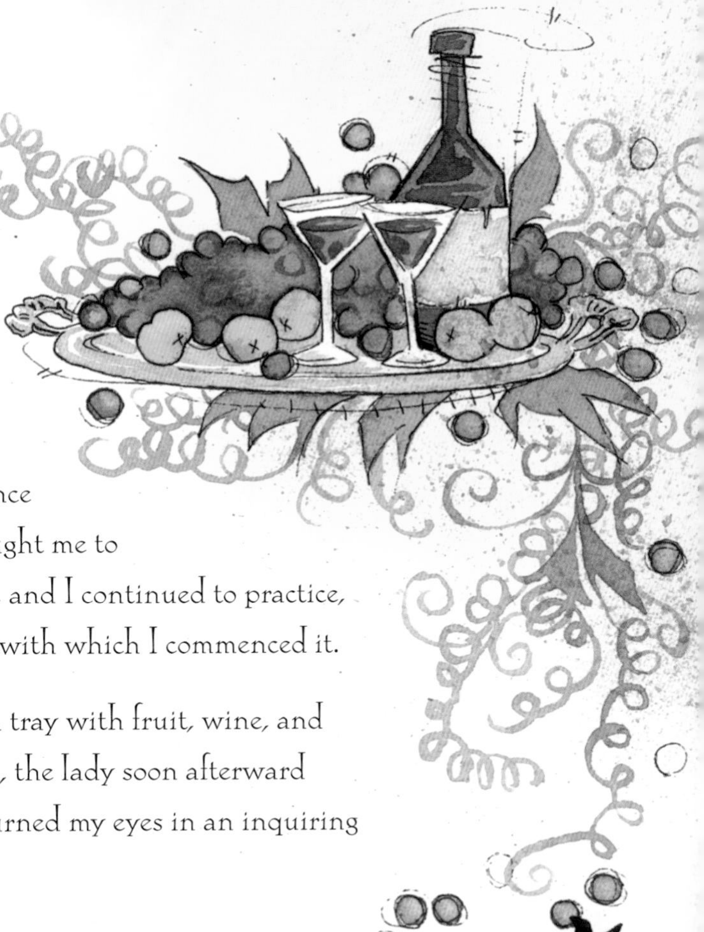

Presently a smart footman brought in a tray with fruit, wine, and other refreshments, of which I partook, the lady soon afterward leaving the room. As she departed I turned my eyes in an inquiring manner toward my host.

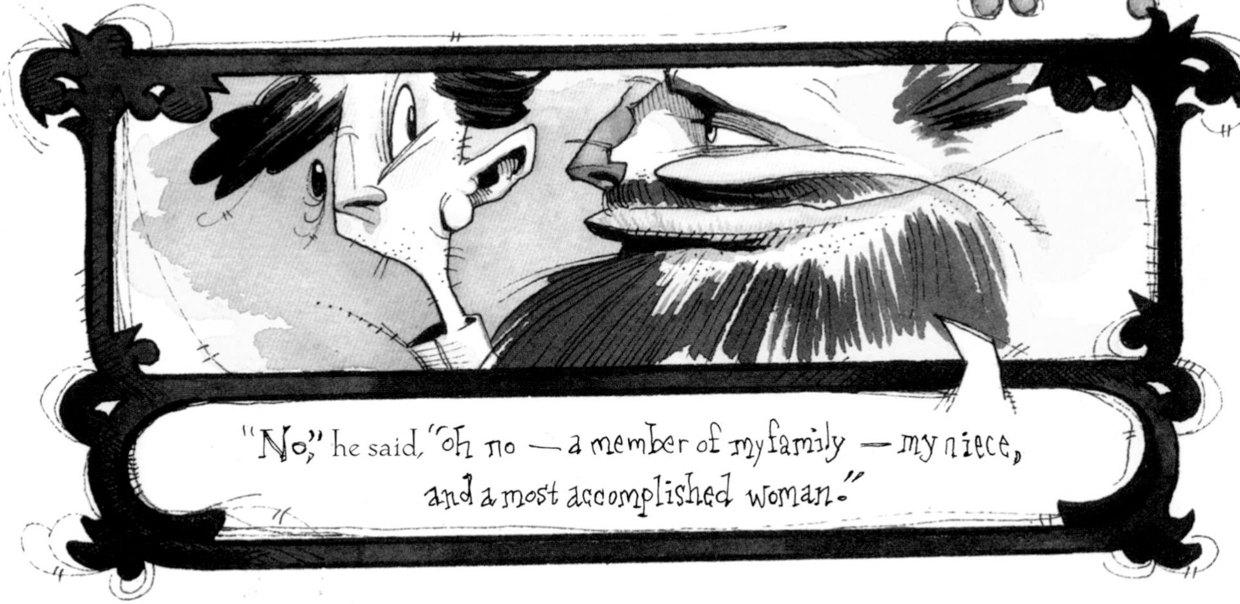
"No," he said, "oh no — a member of my family — my niece,
and a most accomplished woman."

"I beg a thousand pardons," I replied, "but of course you will know how to excuse me. The excellent administration of your affairs here is well understood in Paris, and I thought it just possible, you know—"

"Yes, yes—say no more—or rather it is myself who should thank you for the commendable prudence you have displayed.

"While my former system was in operation, and my patients were permitted the privilege of roaming to and fro at will, they were often aroused to a dangerous frenzy by injudicious persons who called to inspect the house. Hence I was obliged to enforce a rigid system of exclusion; and none obtained access to the premises upon whose discretion I could not rely."

"Do I understand you, then, to say that the 'soothing system' of which I have heard so much, is no longer in force?"

"It is now," he replied, "several weeks since we have concluded to renounce it forever."

"Indeed! You astonish me!"

"We found it, sir," he said, with a sigh, "absolutely necessary to return to the old usages. The danger of the soothing system was appalling; and its advantages have been much overrated. I believe, sir, that in this house it has been given a fair trial, if ever in any. We did every thing that rational humanity could suggest. I am sorry that you could not have paid us a visit at an earlier period, that you might have judged for yourself. But I presume you are conversant with the soothing practice."

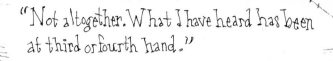

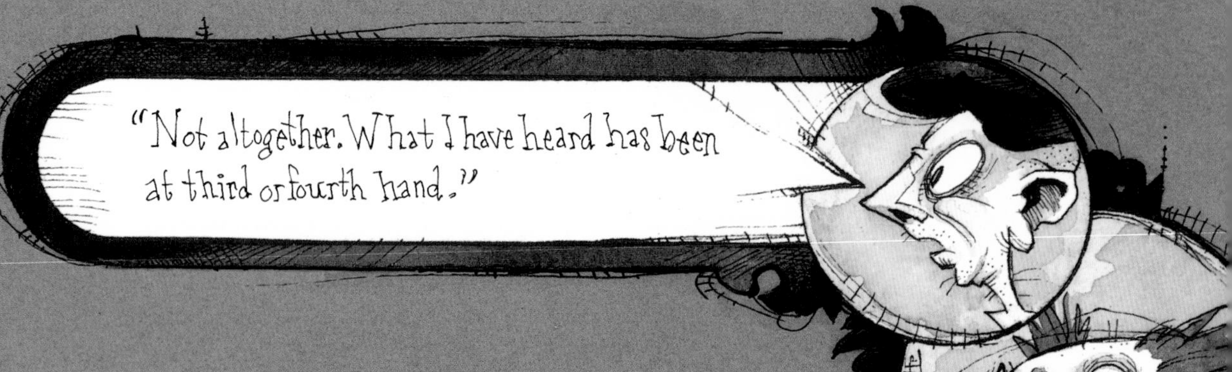

"Not altogether. What I have heard has been at third or fourth hand."

"I may state the system, then, in general terms.... We contradicted no fancies which entered the brains of the mad. On the contrary, we not only indulged but encouraged them; and many of our most permanent cures have been thus effected. There is no argument which so touches the feeble reason of the madman as the reductio ad absurdum. We have had men, for example, who fancied themselves chickens. The cure was to insist upon the thing as a fact — to accuse the patient of stupidity in not sufficiently perceiving it to be a fact — and thus to refuse him any other diet for a week than that which properly appertains to a chicken. In this manner a little corn and gravel were made to perform wonders."

A.

B.

EXAMPLE 1.

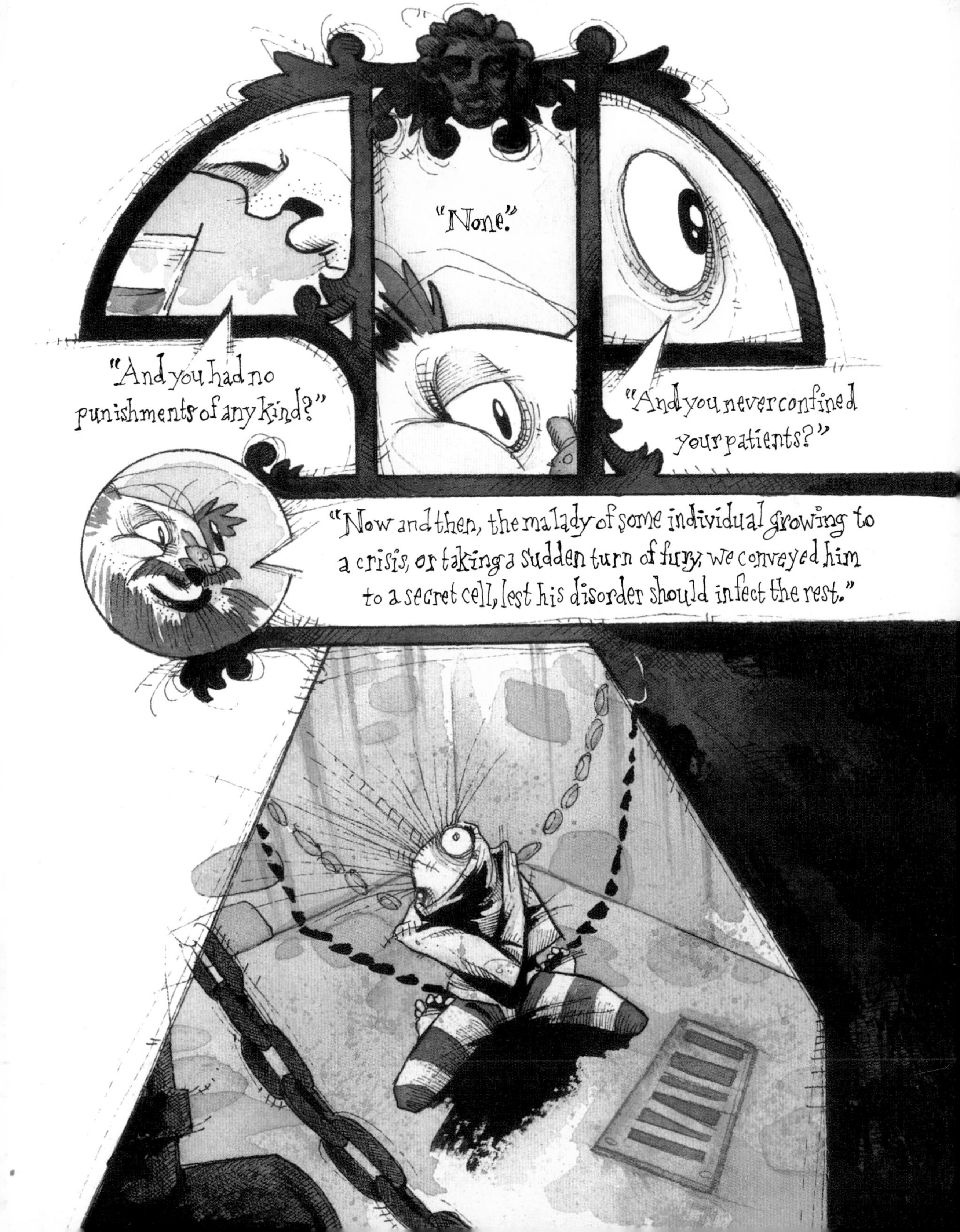
"None."
"And you had no punishments of any kind?"
"And you never confined your patients?"
"Now and then, the malady of some individual growing to a crisis, or taking a sudden turn of fury, we conveyed him to a secret cell, lest his disorder should infect the rest."

"And you have now changed all this — and you think for the better?"

"Decidedly. The system had its disadvantages, and even its dangers."

"I am very much surprised," I said, "for I made sure that, at this moment, no other method of treatment for mania existed in any portion of the country."

"You are young yet, my friend," replied my host. "Believe nothing you hear, and only one-half that you see. Now, about our Maison de Santé, it is clear that some ignoramus has misled you. After dinner, however, I will be happy to take you over the house, and introduce to you a system which, in my opinion, is incomparably the most effectual as yet devised."

"Your own?" I inquired. "One of your own invention?"

"I am proud," he replied, "to acknowledge that it is — at least in some measure."

In this manner I conversed with Monsieur Maillard for an hour or two, during which he showed me the gardens and conservatories of the place.

"I cannot let you see my patients," he said, "just at present. To a sensitive mind there is always more or less of the shocking in such exhibitions; and I do not wish to spoil your appetite for dinner. We will dine.... Then your nerves will be sufficiently steadied."

At six, dinner was announced, and my host conducted me into a large *salle à manger*, where a very numerous company were assembled — twenty-five or thirty in all. They were, apparently, people of rank — certainly of high breeding — although their habiliments, I thought, were extravagantly rich, partaking somewhat too much of the ostentatious finery of the *vielle cour*.

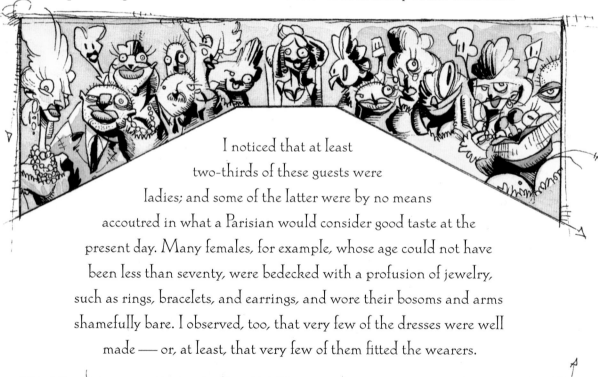

I noticed that at least two-thirds of these guests were ladies; and some of the latter were by no means accoutred in what a Parisian would consider good taste at the present day. Many females, for example, whose age could not have been less than seventy, were bedecked with a profusion of jewelry, such as rings, bracelets, and earrings, and wore their bosoms and arms shamefully bare. I observed, too, that very few of the dresses were well made — or, at least, that very few of them fitted the wearers.

In looking about, I discovered the interesting girl to whom Monsieur Maillard had presented me in the little parlor, but my surprise was great to see her wearing a hoop and farthingale, with high-heeled shoes, and a dirty cap of Brussels lace, so much too large for her that it gave her face a ridiculously diminutive expression. When I had first seen her, she was attired, most becomingly, in deep mourning.

There was an air of oddity, in short, about the dress of the whole party, which, at first, caused me to recur to my original idea of the "soothing system," and to fancy that Monsieur Maillard had been willing to deceive me until after dinner, that I might experience no uncomfortable feelings during the repast, at finding myself dining with lunatics; but I remembered having been informed, in Paris, that the southern provincialists were a peculiarly eccentric people, with a vast number of antiquated notions; and then, too, upon conversing with several members of the company, my apprehensions were immediately and fully dispelled. . . .

There were several active servants in attendance; and, upon a large table, at the farther end of the apartment, were seated seven or eight people with fiddles, fifes, trombones, and a drum. These fellows annoyed me very much during the repast, by an infinite variety of noises, which were intended for music, and which appeared to afford much entertainment to all present, with the exception of myself.

I could not help thinking that there was much of the *bizarre* about everything I saw — but then the world is made up of all kinds of persons, with all modes of thought, and all sorts of conventional customs. So I took my seat very coolly at the right hand of my host, and did justice to the good cheer set before me.

The conversation, in the meantime, was spirited. I soon found that nearly all the company were well educated; and my host was quite willing to speak of his position as superintendent of a Maison de Santé; and, indeed, the topic of lunacy was, much to my surprise, a favorite one with all present. A great many amusing stories were told.

"We had a fellow here once," said a fat little gentleman, who sat at my right — "a fellow that fancied himself a teapot; and, by the way, is it not especially singular how often this particular crotchet has entered the brain of the lunatic? There is scarcely an insane asylum in France which cannot supply a human teapot. Our gentleman was a Britannia-ware teapot and was careful to polish himself every morning with buckskin and whiting."

"And then," said a tall man just opposite, "we had here, not long ago, a person who had taken it into his head that he was a donkey — which, allegorically speaking, you will say, was quite true. For a long time he would eat nothing but thistles; but of this idea we soon cured him by insisting upon his eating nothing else. Then he was perpetually kicking out his heels — so — so —"

"Mr. De Kock! I will thank you to behave yourself!" here interrupted an old lady, who sat next to the speaker. "Please keep your feet to yourself! Is it necessary, pray, to illustrate a remark? Our friend here can surely comprehend you without all this. Upon my word, you are nearly as great a donkey as the poor unfortunate imagined himself."

"Mille pardons! Ma'm'selle!" replied Monsieur De Kock, thus addressed. "I had no intention of offending."

Here Monsieur De Kock bowed low, kissed his hand with much ceremony, and took wine with Ma'm'selle Laplace.

"Allow me, mon ami," now said Monsieur Maillard, addressing myself, "allow me to send you a morsel of this veal à la St. Menehoult — you will find it particularly fine."

At this instant three sturdy waiters had just succeeded in depositing safely upon the table an enormous dish, or trencher, containing a small calf roasted whole, and set upon its knees, with an apple in its mouth, as is the English fashion of dressing a hare.

"Thank you, no," I replied, "to say the truth, I am not particularly partial to veal à la St.——what is it?—for I do not find that it altogether agrees with me. I will change my plate, however, and try some of the rabbit."

"Pierre," cried the host, "change this gentleman's plate, and give him a side piece of this rabbit au-chat."

"This what?" said I.

47

"Why, thank you — upon second thoughts, no.
I will just help myself to some of the ham."

"And then," said a cadaverous-looking personage, near the foot of the table,
taking up the thread of the conversation where it had been broken off —

" and then, we had a patient, once upon a time, who very pertinaciously
maintained himself to be a Cordova cheese, and went about, with a knife in his
hand, soliciting his friends to try a small slice from the middle of his leg."

"He was a great fool," interposed someone, "but not to be compared with a certain individual who took himself for a bottle of champagne, and always went off with a pop and a fizz, in this fashion."

Here the speaker, very rudely, as I thought, put his right thumb in his left cheek, withdrew it with a sound resembling the popping of a cork, and then, by a dexterous movement of the tongue upon the teeth, created a sharp hissing and fizzing, which lasted for several minutes, in imitation of the frothing of champagne. This behavior, I saw plainly, was not very pleasing to Monsieur Maillard; but that gentleman said nothing, and the conversation was resumed by a very lean little man in a big wig.

"And then there was an ignoramus," said he, "who mistook himself for a frog, which, by the way, he resembled in no little degree. I wish you could have seen him, sir," — here the speaker addressed myself —

"Sir, if that man was not a frog, I can only observe that it is a pity he was not. His croak thus — o-o-o-o-gh — o-o-o-o-gh! — was the finest note in the world — B flat; and when he put his elbows upon the table thus — after taking a glass or two of wine — and distended his mouth, thus, and rolled up his eyes, thus, and winked them with excessive rapidity, thus, why then, sir you would have been lost in admiration of the genius of the man."

"I have no doubt of it," I said.

"And then there was Jules Desoulières, who was a very singular genius, indeed, and went mad with the idea that he was a pumpkin. He persecuted the cook to make him up into pies — a thing which the cook indignantly refused to do. For my part, I am by no means sure that a pumpkin pie à la Desoulières would not have been very capital eating indeed!"

"You astonish me!" said I; and I looked inquisitively at Monsieur Maillard.

"Ha! ha ha!" said that gentleman — "he! he! he! — hi! hi! hi! — ho! ho! ho! — hu! hu! hu! hu! — very good, indeed! You must not be astonished, mon ami; our friend here is a wit — a drôle — you must not understand him to a letter."

51

"But then," cried the old lady, at the top of her voice, "your Monsieur Boullard was a madman, and a very silly madman at best; for who, allow me to ask you, ever heard of a human teetotum? The thing is absurd. Madame Joyeuse was a more sensible person. She had a crotchet, but it was instinct with common sense, and it gave pleasure to all who had the honor of her acquaintance. She found, upon mature deliberation, that, by some accident, she had been turned into a chicken cock; but, as such, she behaved with propriety. She flapped her wings with prodigious effect — so — so — so — and, as for her crow, it was delicious! Cock-a-doodle-doo! — Cock-a-doodle-doo! — cock-a-doodle-de-doo-doo-dooo-do-o-o-o-o-o-o!"

"Madame Joyeuse, I will thank you to behave yourself!" here interrupted our host, very angrily. "You can either conduct yourself as a lady should do, or you can quit the table forthwith — take your choice."

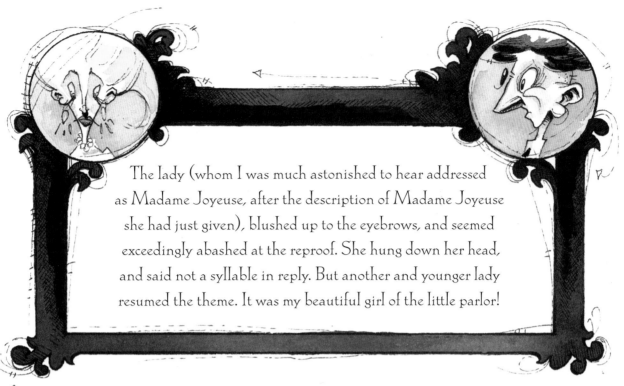

The lady (whom I was much astonished to hear addressed as Madame Joyeuse, after the description of Madame Joyeuse she had just given), blushed up to the eyebrows, and seemed exceedingly abashed at the reproof. She hung down her head, and said not a syllable in reply. But another and younger lady resumed the theme. It was my beautiful girl of the little parlor!

"Oh, Madame Joyeuse *was* a fool!" she exclaimed. "But there was much sound sense, in the opinion of Eugénie Salsafette. She was a very beautiful and painfully modest young lady, who thought the ordinary mode of habiliment indecent, and wished to dress herself, always, by getting outside instead of inside of her clothes. It is a thing very easily done, after all. You have only to do so — and then so — so — so — and then so — so — so — and then —"

"Mon dieu! Ma'm'selle Salsafette!"

here cried a dozen voices at once. "What *are* you about? — forbear! — that is sufficient! — we see, very plainly, how it is done! — hold! hold!"

And several persons were already leaping from their seats to withhold Ma'm'selle Salsafette from putting herself upon a par with the Medicean Venus, when the point was very effectually and suddenly accomplished by a series of loud screams, or yells, from some portion of the main body of the château.

My nerves were very much affected, indeed, by these yells; but the rest of the company I really pitied. I never saw any set of reasonable people so thoroughly frightened in my life. They all grew as pale as corpses, and, shrinking within their seats, sat quivering and gibbering with terror, and listening for the repetition of the sound.

It came again — louder and seemingly nearer — and then a third time *very* loud, and then a fourth time with a vigor evidently diminished. At this apparent dying away of the noise, the spirits of the company were immediately regained, and all was life and anecdote as before. I now ventured to inquire the cause of the disturbance.

"A mere bagatelle," said Monsieur Maillard. "We are used to these things, and care really very little about them. The lunatics, every now and then, get up a howl in concert; one starting another, as is sometimes the case with a bevy of dogs at night. It occasionally happens, however, that the concerto yells are succeeded by a simultaneous effort at breaking loose, when, of course, some little danger is to be apprehended."

"And how many have you in charge?"

"At present we have not more than ten altogether."

"Principally females, I presume?"

"Oh, no — every one of them men, and stout fellows, too, I can tell you."

"Indeed! I have always understood that the majority of lunatics were of the gentler sex."

"It is generally so, but not always. Some time ago, there were about twenty-seven patients here; and, of that number, no less than eighteen were women; but, lately, matters have changed very much, as you see."

"Yes — have changed very much, as you see!" chimed in the whole company at once.

"Hold your tongues, every one of you!" said my host, in a great rage.

Whereupon the whole company maintained a dead silence one lady obeyed Monsieur Maillard to the letter, and thrusting out her tongue, which was an excessively long one, held it with both hands.

"And this gentlewoman," said I, to Monsieur Maillard, bending over and addressing him in a whisper, "this good lady who gives us the cock-a-doodle-de-doo—she, I presume, is harmless— quite harmless, eh?"

"Harmless!" ejaculated he, in unfeigned surprise. "Why — why, what can you mean?"

"Only slightly touched?" said I, touching my head.

"Mon dieu! what is it you imagine? This lady, my old friend Madame Joyeuse, is as absolutely sane as myself. She has her little eccentricities, to be sure — but then, you know, all old women — all very old women — are more or less eccentric!"

"To be sure," said I, "to be sure — and then the rest of these ladies and gentlemen —"

"Are my friends and keepers," interrupted Monsieur Maillard, drawing himself up with hauteur, "my very good friends and assistants."

"What! All of them?" I asked.

"Assuredly," he said, "we could not do at all without the women; they are the best lunatic nurses in the world."

"To be sure," said I, "to be sure! They behave a little odd, eh? Don't you think so?"

"Odd! Queer! Why, do you really think so? We are not very prudish, to be sure, here in the South — do pretty much as we please — enjoy life, and all that sort of thing, you know—"

"To be sure," said I, "to be sure. By-the-by, monsieur, did I understand you to say that the system you have adopted, in place of the celebrated soothing system, was one of very rigorous severity?"

"By no means. Our confinement is necessarily close, but the treatment — the medical treatment, I mean — is rather agreeable to the patients."

"And the new system is one of your own invention?"

"Not altogether. Some portions of it are referable to Doctor Tarr, of whom you have, necessarily, heard; and, again, there are modifications in my plan which I am happy to acknowledge as belonging of right to the celebrated Fether, with whom, if I mistake not, you have the honor of an intimate acquaintance."

"I am quite ashamed to confess," I replied, "that I have never even heard the names of either gentleman before."

"Good heavens!" ejaculated my host, drawing back his chair abruptly and uplifting his hands. "I surely do not hear you aright! You did not intend to say, eh, that you had never heard either of the learned Doctor Tarr or of the celebrated Professor Fether?"

I replied, "I feel humbled to the dust, not to be acquainted with the works of these, no doubt, extraordinary men. I will seek out their writings forthwith. Monsieur Maillard, you have really — I must confess it — you have *really* — made me ashamed of myself!"

And this was the fact.

"Say no more, my good young friend," he said kindly, pressing my hand, "join me now in a glass of Sauterne."

We drank. The company followed our example, without stint. They chatted — they jested — they laughed — they perpetrated a thousand absurdities — the fiddles shrieked — the drum row-de-dowed — the trombones bellowed like so many brazen bulls of Phalaris — and the whole scene, growing gradually worse and worse, as the wines gained the ascendancy, became at length a sort of pandemonium *in petto*. A word spoken in an ordinary key stood no more chance of being heard than the voice of a fish from the bottom of Niagara Falls.

"And, sir," said I, screaming in his ear, "you mentioned something before dinner about the danger incurred in the old system of soothing. How is that?"

"Yes," he replied, "there was, occasionally, very great danger indeed. There is no accounting for the caprices of madmen; and, in my opinion, as well as in that of Doctor Tarr and Professor Fether, it is *never* safe to permit them to run at large unattended. A lunatic may be 'soothed,' as it is called, for a time, but, in the end, he is very apt to become obstreperous. His cunning, too, is proverbial, and great. If he has a project in view, he conceals his design with a marvellous wisdom; and the dexterity with which he counterfeits sanity, presents one of the most singular problems in the study of mind. When a madman appears *thoroughly* sane, indeed, it is high time to put him in a straitjacket."

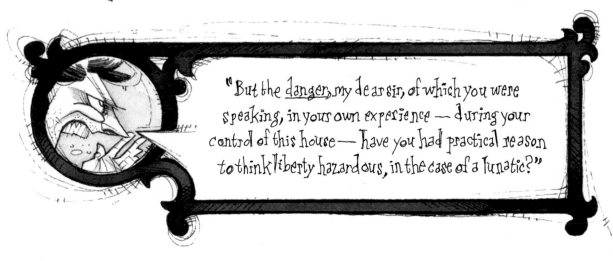

"But the danger, my dear sir, of which you were speaking, in your own experience — during your control of this house — have you had practical reason to think liberty hazardous, in the case of a lunatic?"

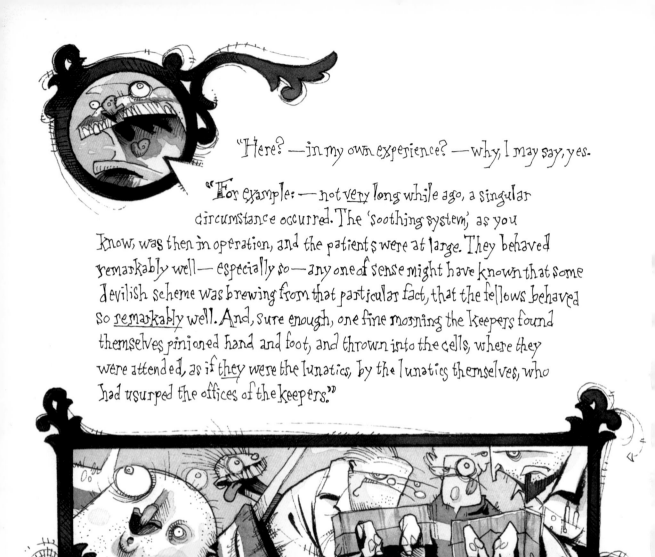

"Here? —in my own experience? —why, I may say, yes.

"For example: — not very long while ago, a singular circumstance occurred. The 'soothing system', as you know, was then in operation, and the patients were at large. They behaved remarkably well — especially so — any one of sense might have known that some devilish scheme was brewing from that particular fact, that the fellows behaved so remarkably well. And, sure enough, one fine morning the keepers found themselves pinioned hand and foot, and thrown into the cells, where they were attended, as if they were the lunatics, by the lunatics themselves, who had usurped the offices of the keepers."

"You don't tell me so! I never heard of anything so absurd in my life!"

"Fact — it all came to pass by means of a stupid fellow — a lunatic — who, by some means, had taken it into his head that he had invented a better system of government than any ever heard of before —

"of lunatic government, I mean. He wished to give his invention a trial, I suppose — and so he persuaded the rest of the patients to join him in a conspiracy for the overthrow of the reigning powers."

"And he succeeded?"

"No doubt of it. The keepers and kept were soon made to exchange places. Not that exactly either — for the madmen had been free, but the keepers were shut up in cells forthwith, and treated, I am sorry to say, in a very cavalier manner."

"But I presume a counter revolution was soon effected. This condition of things could not have long existed. The country people in the neighborhood — visitors coming to see the establishment — would have given the alarm."

"There you are out. The head rebel was too cunning for that. He admitted no visitors at all — with the exception, one day, of a very stupid-looking young gentleman of whom he had no reason to be afraid. He let him in to see the place — just by way of variety — to have a little fun with him. As soon as he had gammoned him sufficiently, he let him out and sent him about his business."

"And how long, then, did the madmen reign?"

"Oh, a very long time, indeed — a month certainly — how much longer I can't precisely say. In the meantime, the lunatics had a jolly season of it. They doffed their own shabby clothes and made free with the family wardrobe and jewels. The cellars of the château were well stocked with wine; and these madmen are just the devils that know how to drink it. They lived well, I can tell you."

"And the treatment — what was the particular species of treatment which the leader of the rebels put into operation?"

"Why, as for that, a madman is not necessarily a fool, as I have already observed; and it is my honest opinion that his treatment was a much better treatment than that which it superceded. It was a very capital system indeed — simple — neat — no trouble at all — in fact, it was delicious."

Here my host's observations were cut short by another series of yells, of the same character as those which had previously disconcerted us. This time, however, they seemed to proceed from persons rapidly approaching.

"Gracious Heavens!"

I ejaculated.

"The lunatics have most undoubtedly broken loose."

"I very much fear it is so," replied Monsieur Maillard, becoming excessively pale.

He had scarcely finished the sentence, before loud shouts and imprecations were heard beneath the windows; and, immediately afterward, it became evident that some persons outside were endeavoring to gain entrance into the room. The door was beaten with what appeared to be a sledgehammer, and the shutters were wrenched and shaken with prodigious violence.

Monsieur Maillard, to my astonishment, threw himself under the sideboard. I had expected more resolution at his hands.

Hearing an incredible popping and fizzing of champagne, I discovered at length, that it proceeded from the person who performed the bottle of that delicate drink during dinner. And then, again, the frog-man croaked away as if the salvation of his soul depended upon every note that he uttered. And, in the midst of all this, the continuous braying of a donkey arose over all. As for my old friend, Madame Joyeuse, I really could have wept for the poor lady, she appeared so terribly perplexed. All she did, however, was to stand up in a corner, by the fireplace, and sing out incessantly, at the top of her voice, "Cock-a-doodle-de-doooooo!"

And now came the climax — the catastrophe of the drama. As no resistance, beyond whooping and yelling and cock-a-doodling, was offered to the encroachments of the party without, the ten windows were very speedily broken in.

But I shall never forget the emotions of wonder and horror with which I gazed, when, leaping through these windows, and down among us *pêle-mêle*, fighting, stamping, scratching, and howling, there rushed a perfect army of what I took to be chimpanzees, orangutans, or big black baboons . . .

I received a terrible beating — after which I rolled under a sofa and lay still.

After lying there some fifteen minutes, I came to same satisfactory dénouement of this tragedy. Monsieur Maillard, it appeared, in giving me the account of the lunatic who had excited his fellows to rebellion, had been merely relating his own exploits.

This gentleman had, indeed, some two or three years before, been the superintendent of the establishment, but grew crazy himself, and so became a patient. This fact was unknown to the traveling companion who introduced me.

The keepers, ten in number, having been suddenly overpowered, were first well tarred, then carefully feathered, and then shut up in underground cells. They had been so imprisoned for more than a month, during which period Monsieur Maillard had generously allowed them not only the tar and feathers (which constituted his "system"), but some bread and abundance of water. At length, one escaping through a sewer, gave freedom to all the rest.

I have only to add that, although I have searched every library in Europe for the works of Doctor Tarr and Professor Fether, I have, up to the present day, utterly failed in my endeavors at procuring an edition.

The Oblong Box

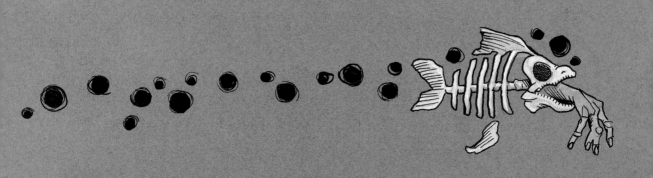

Some years ago, I engaged passage from Charleston, SC, to the city of New York, in the fine packet ship *Independence*, Captain Hardy. We were to sail on the fifteenth of the month (June), weather permitting; and, on the fourteenth, I went onboard to arrange some matters in my stateroom.

I found that we were to have a great many passengers. Among other names, I was rejoiced to see that of Mr. Cornelius Wyatt, a young artist, for whom I entertained feelings of warm friendship. He had been with me a fellow student at C — University, where we were very much together. He had the ordinary temperament of genius, and was a compound of misanthropy, sensibility, and enthusiasm. To these qualities he united the warmest and truest heart which ever beat in a human bosom.

I observed that his name was carded upon *three* staterooms; he had engaged passage for himself, wife, and two sisters — his own.

The staterooms were sufficiently roomy, and each had two berths, one above the other. These berths, to be sure, were so exceedingly narrow as to be insufficient for more than one person; still, I could not comprehend why there were *three* staterooms for these four persons. I was in one of those moody frames of mind which make a man abnormally inquisitive about trifles. And I confess, with shame, that I busied myself in a variety of ill-bred and preposterous conjectures about this matter of the supernumerary stateroom. It was no business of mine, to be sure, but with none the less pertinacity did I occupy myself in attempts to resolve the enigma. At last I reached a conclusion.

"It is a servant, of course," I said. "What a fool I am, not sooner to have thought of so obvious a solution!"

And then I again repaired to the list — but here I saw distinctly that *no* servant was to come with the party; although, in fact, it had been the original design to bring one — for the words "and servant" had been first written and then overscored.

"Oh, extra baggage, to be sure," I now said to myself. "Something he wishes not to be put in the hold — something to be kept under his own eye —

"ah, I have it — a painting — and this is what he has been bargaining about with Nicolino." This idea satisfied me, and I dismissed my curiosity for the nonce.

Wyatt's two sisters I knew very well, and most amiable and clever girls they were. His wife he had newly married, and I had never yet seen her.

He had often talked about her in my presence, however, and in his usual style of enthusiasm. He described her as of surpassing beauty, wit, and accomplishment. I was, therefore, quite anxious to make her acquaintance.

On the day in which I visited the ship (the fourteenth), Wyatt and party were also to visit it — so the captain informed me — and I waited onboard an hour longer than I had designed, in hope of being presented to the bride, but then an apology came.

"Mrs. W. was a little indisposed, and would decline coming onboard until tomorrow, at the hour of sailing."

Wyatt's party arrived in about ten minutes after myself. There were the two sisters, the bride, and the artist — the latter in one of his customary fits of moody misanthropy.

I was too well used to these, however, to pay them any especial attention. He did not even introduce me to his wife — this courtesy devolving upon his sister Marian — a very sweet and intelligent girl, who, in a few hurried words, made us acquainted.

Mrs. Wyatt had been closely veiled; and when she raised her veil I confess that I was very profoundly astonished. The truth is, I could not help regarding Mrs. Wyatt as a decidedly plain-looking woman. If not positively ugly, she was not, I think, very far from it.

She was dressed, however, in exquisite taste — and then I had no doubt that she had captivated my friend's heart by the more enduring graces of the intellect and soul. She said very few words and passed at once into her stateroom, with Mr. W.

My old inquisitiveness now returned. There was *no* servant — *that* was a settled point. I looked, therefore, for the extra baggage.

After some delay, a cart arrived at the wharf, with an oblong pine box, which was everything that seemed to be expected. Immediately upon its arrival we made sail, and in a short time were safely over the bar and standing out to sea.

A.

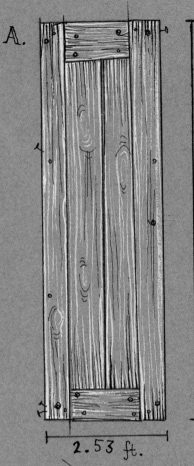

5.10 ft.

2.53 ft.

The box in question was, as I say, oblong. It was about six feet in length, by two and a half in breadth. Now this shape was *peculiar*; and no sooner had I seen it, than I took credit to myself for the accuracy of my guessing. I had reached the conclusion, it will be remembered, that the extra baggage would prove to be pictures, or at least a picture; for I knew he had been for several weeks in conference with Nicolino. And now here was a box, which, from its shape, *could* possibly contain nothing in the world but a copy of Leonardo's *Last Supper*, and a copy of this very *Last Supper*, done by Rubini the younger, at Florence, I had known, for some time, to be in the possession of Nicolino.

B.

I chuckled excessively when I thought of my acumen. It was the first time I had ever known Wyatt to keep from me any of his artistical secrets. But here he evidently intended to steal a march upon me and smuggle a fine picture to New York, under my very nose; expecting me to know nothing of the matter. I resolved to quiz him well, now and hereafter.

One thing, however, annoyed me no little. The box did *not* go into the extra stateroom. It was deposited in Wyatt's own; and there, too, it remained, occupying very nearly the whole of the floor — no doubt to the exceeding discomfort of the artist and his wife — this the more especially as the tar or paint with which it was lettered in sprawling capitals, emitted a strong, disagreeable odor. On the lid were painted the words — *"Mrs. Adelaide Curtis, Albany, New York. Charge of Cornelius Wyatt, Esq. This side up. To be handled with care."*

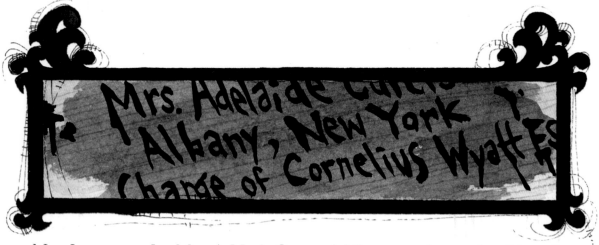

Now I was aware that Mrs. Adelaide Curtis, of Albany, was the artist's wife's mother, but then I looked upon the whole address of a mystification, intended especially for myself. I made up my mind, of course, that the box and contents would never get farther north than the studio of my misanthropic friend in Chambers Street, New York.

For the first three or four days we had fine weather, although the wind was dead ahead; having chopped round to the northward, immediately upon our losing sight of the coast. The passengers were, consequently, in high spirits, and disposed to be social.

I must except, however, Wyatt and his sisters, who behaved stiffly. Wyatt's conduct I did not so much regard. He was gloomy, even beyond his usual habit — in fact, he was morose — but in him I was prepared for eccentricity. For the sisters, however, I could make no excuse. They secluded themselves in their staterooms during the greater part of the passage, and absolutely refused, although I repeatedly urged them, to hold communication with any person onboard.

Mrs. Wyatt herself was far more agreeable. That is to say, she was chatty; and to be chatty is no slight recommendation at sea. She became excessively intimate with most of the ladies; and, to my profound astonishment, evinced no equivocal disposition to coquet with the men. She amused us all very much. I say "amused" — and scarcely know how to explain myself.

The truth is, I soon found that Mrs. W. was far oftener laughed *at* than *with*. The gentlemen said little about her; but the ladies, in a little while, pronounced her "a good-hearted thing, rather indifferent-looking, totally uneducated, and decidedly vulgar."

The great wonder was how Wyatt had been entrapped into such a match. Wealth was the general solution — but this I knew to be no solution at all. "He had married," he said, "for love, and for love only; and his bride was far more than worthy of his love."

When I thought of these expressions, on the part of
my friend, I confess that I felt indescribably puzzled.
Could it be possible that he was taking leave of his
senses? *He,* so refined, so intellectual, so fastidious,
with so exquisite a perception of the faulty and so
keen an appreciation of the beautiful! To be sure,
the lady seemed especially fond of *him* — particularly
so in his absence — when she made herself ridiculous
by frequent quotations of what had been said by her
"beloved husband, Mr. Wyatt." In the meantime it
was observed by all onboard that he avoided *her* in
the most pointed manner, and, for the most part,
shut himself up alone in his stateroom.

My conclusion, from what I saw and heard, was that the artist had been induced to unite himself with a person altogether beneath him, and that the natural result — entire and speedy disgust — had ensued. I pitied him from the bottom of my heart — but could not, for that reason, quite forgive his incommunicativeness in the matter of the *Last Supper*. For this I resolved to have my revenge.

One day he came upon deck, and, taking his arm as had been my wont, I sauntered with him backward and forward. His gloom, however, seemed entirely unabated. I ventured a jest or two, and he made a sickening attempt at a smile. Poor fellow — as I thought of *his wife*, I wondered that he could have heart to put on even the semblance of mirth. I determined to commence a series of covert insinuations, or innuendoes, about the oblong box — just by way of letting him perceive, gradually, that I was *not* altogether the butt, or victim, of his little bit of pleasant mystification.

I said something about the "peculiar shape of *that* box"; and, as I spoke the words, I smiled knowingly, winked, and touched him gently with my forefinger in the ribs.

The manner in which Wyatt received this harmless pleasantry convinced me, at once, that he was mad.

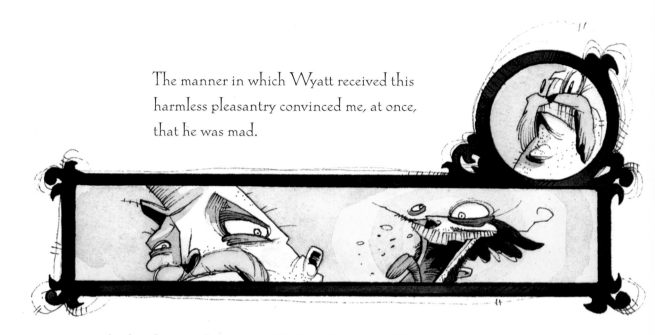

At first he stared at me as if he found it impossible to comprehend the witticism of my remark; but as its point seemed slowly to make its way into his brain, his eyes seemed protruding from their sockets. Then he grew very red — then hideously pale — then, as if highly amused with what I had insinuated, he began a loud and boisterous laugh, which, to my astonishment, he kept up, with gradually increasing vigor, for ten minutes or more. In conclusion, he fell flat and heavily upon the deck. When I ran to uplift him, to all appearance he utterly was *dead*.

I called for assistance, and, with much difficulty,
we brought him to himself. Upon reviving,
he spoke incoherently for some time.

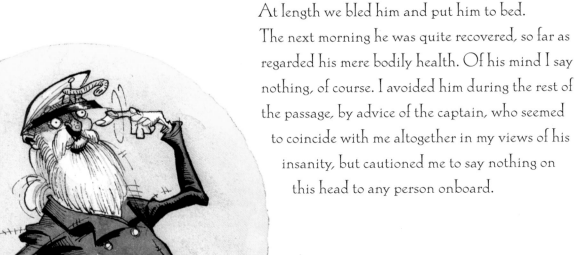

At length we bled him and put him to bed.
The next morning he was quite recovered, so far as
regarded his mere bodily health. Of his mind I say
nothing, of course. I avoided him during the rest of
the passage, by advice of the captain, who seemed
to coincide with me altogether in my views of his
insanity, but cautioned me to say nothing on
this head to any person onboard.

Several circumstances occurred immediately after this fit of Wyatt's, which contributed to heighten the curiosity with which I was already possessed. Among other things, this: I drank too much strong green tea and slept ill at night.

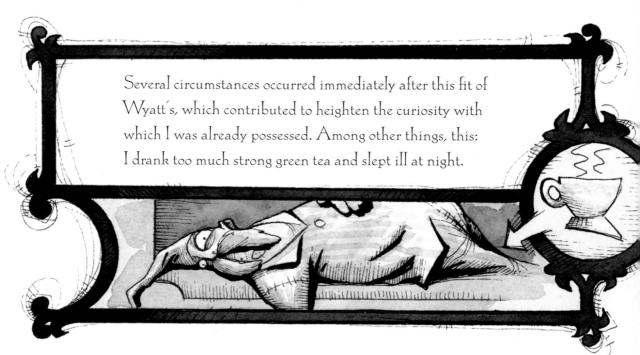

Well, during two nights (*not* consecutive), while I lay awake, I clearly saw Mrs. W. about eleven o'clock upon each night, steal cautiously from the stateroom of Mr. W. and enter the extra room, where she remained until daybreak, when she was called by her husband and went back. That they were virtually separated was clear. They had separate apartments — no doubt in contemplation of a more permanent divorce; and here, after all, I thought, was the mystery of the extra stateroom.

There was another circumstance, too, which interested me much. During the two wakeful nights in question, and immediately after the disappearance of Mrs. Wyatt into the extra stateroom, I was attracted by certain singular, cautious, subdued noises in that of her husband.

They were sounds occasioned by the artist in prying open the oblong box, by means of a chisel and mallet — the latter being apparently muffled, or deadened, by some soft woollen or cotton substance in which its head was enveloped.

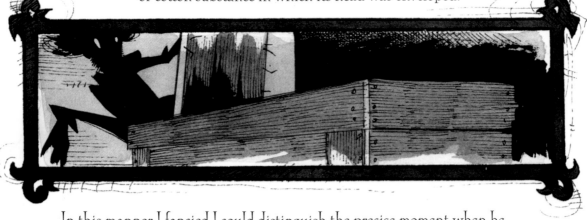

In this manner I fancied I could distinguish the precise moment when he fairly disengaged the lid — also, that I could determine when he removed it altogether, and when he deposited it upon the lower berth in his room — this latter point I knew, for example, by certain slight taps which the lid made in striking against the wooden edges of the berth.

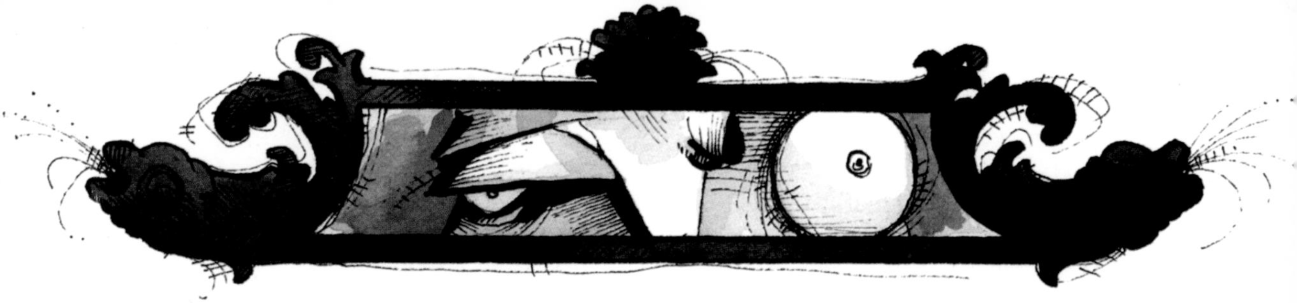

After this there was a dead stillness, and I heard nothing more, upon either occasion, until nearly daybreak; unless, perhaps, I may mention a low sobbing, or murmuring sound, so very much suppressed as to be nearly inaudible — if, indeed, the whole of this latter noise were not rather produced by my own imagination. I say it seemed to *resemble* sobbing or sighing — but, of course, it could not have been either. I rather think it was a ringing in my own ears. Mr. Wyatt, no doubt, was merely indulging in one of his fits of artistic enthusiasm. He had opened his oblong box, in order to feast his eyes on the pictorial treasure within. There was nothing in this, however, to make him *sob*. I repeat, therefore, that it must have been, simply, a freak of my own fancy, distempered by good Captain Hardy's green tea. Just before dawn, on each of the two nights of which I speak, I distinctly heard Mr. Wyatt replace the lid upon the oblong box, and force the nails into their old places, by means of the muffled mallet. Having done this, he issued from his stateroom, fully dressed, and proceeded to call Mrs. W. from hers.

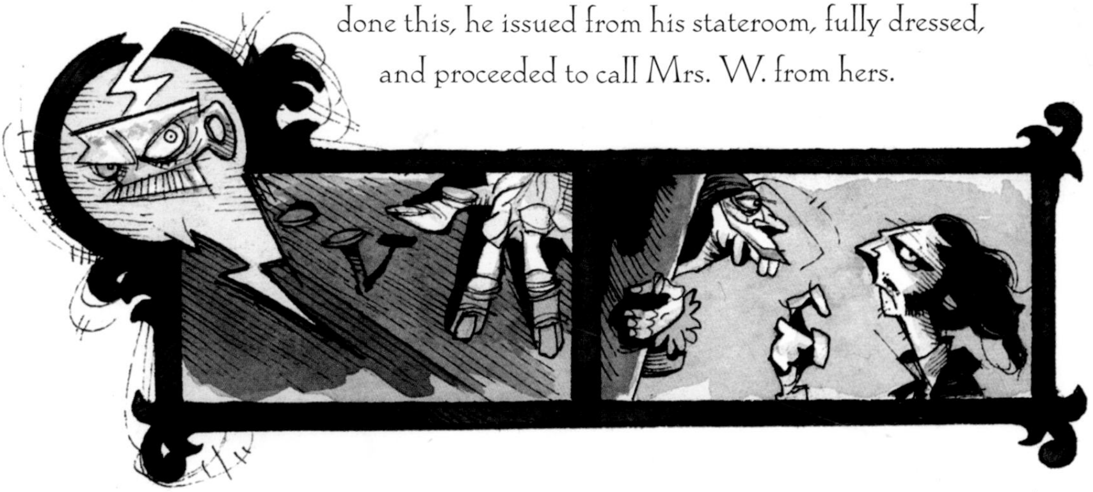

We had been at sea seven days, and were now off Cape Hatteras, when there came a tremendously heavy blow from the southwest. Everything was made snug, alow and aloft; and as the wind steadily freshened, we lay to, at length, under spanker and foretopsail, both double reefed.

In this trim we rode safely enough for forty-eight hours — the ship proving herself an excellent sea boat, in many respects. At the end of this period, however, the gale had freshened into a hurricane, and our after-sail split into ribbons, bringing us so much in the trough of the water that we shipped several prodigious seas, one immediately after the other. By this accident we lost three men overboard, with the caboose, and nearly the whole of the larboard bulwarks. Scarcely had we recovered our senses, before the foretopsail went into shreds, when we got up a storm stay-sail, and with this did pretty well for some hours, the ship heading the sea much more steadily than before.

The gale still held on, however, and we saw no signs of its abating. The rigging was found to be ill-fitted and greatly strained; and on the third day of the blow, about five in the afternoon, our mizzen-mast, in a heavy lurch to windward, went by the board. For an hour or more, we tried in vain to get rid of it, and, before we had succeeded, the carpenter came aft and announced four feet of water in the hold. To add to our dilemma, we found the pumps choked and nearly useless.

All was now confusion and despair — but an effort was made to
lighten the ship by throwing overboard as much of her cargo as could
be reached and by cutting away the two masts that remained. This we
at last accomplished — but we were still unable to do anything at
the pumps; and, in the meantime, the leak gained on us very fast.

At sundown, the gale had sensibly
diminished in violence, and, as the sea
went down with it, we still entertained
faint hopes of saving ourselves in the
boats. At eight p.m., the clouds broke
away to windward, and we had the
advantage of a full moon — a piece of
good fortune which saved wonderfully
to cheer our drooping spirits.

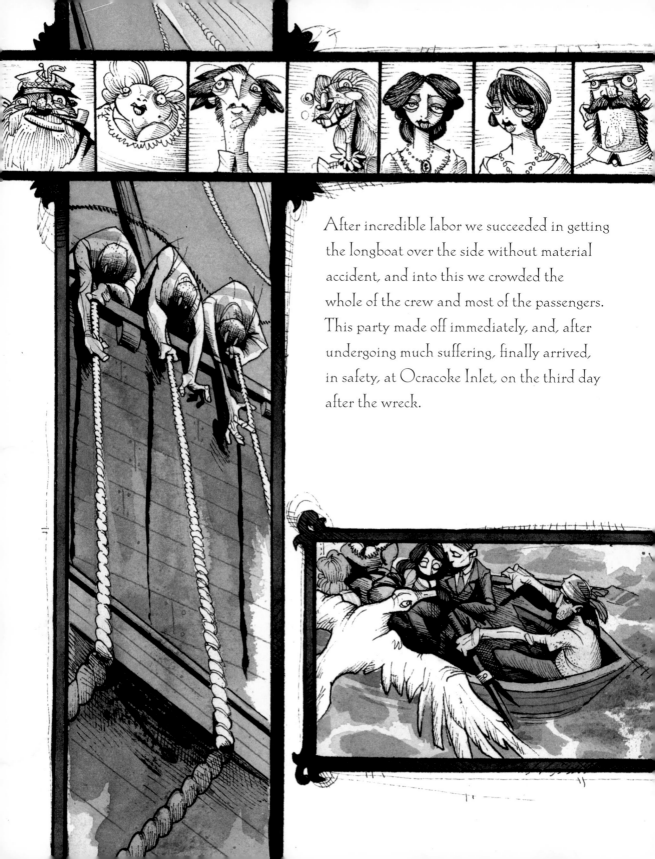

After incredible labor we succeeded in getting the longboat over the side without material accident, and into this we crowded the whole of the crew and most of the passengers. This party made off immediately, and, after undergoing much suffering, finally arrived, in safety, at Ocracoke Inlet, on the third day after the wreck.

Fourteen passengers, with the captain, remained onboard, resolving to trust their fortunes to the jolly boat at the stern. We lowered it without difficulty. It contained, when afloat, the captain and his wife; Mr. Wyatt and party; a Mexican officer, wife, four children; and myself, with a valet.

We had no room, of course, for anything except a few positively necessary instruments, some provisions, and the clothes upon our backs. No one had thought of even attempting to save anything more. What must have been the astonishment of all, then, when, having proceeded a few fathoms from the ship, Mr. Wyatt stood up in the stern sheets, and coolly demanded of Captain Hardy that the boat should be put back for the purpose of taking in his oblong box!

"Sit down, Mr. Wyatt," replied the captain, somewhat sternly. "You will capsize us if you do not sit quite still."

"The box!" vociferated Mr. Wyatt, still standing. "The box, I say! Captain Hardy, you cannot, you will not refuse me. Its weight will be but a trifle — it is nothing — mere nothing. By the mother who bore you — for the love of heaven — by your hope of salvation, I implore you to put back for the box!"

The captain, for a moment, seemed touched by the earnest appeal of the artist, but he regained his stern composure, and said:

"Mr. Wyatt, you are mad. I cannot listen to you. Sit down, I say, or you will swamp the boat. Stay—hold him — seize him! — he is about to spring overboard! There — I knew it — he is over!"

As the captain said this, Mr. Wyatt, in fact, sprang from the boat, and, as we were yet in the lee of the wreck, succeeded, by almost superhuman exertion, in getting hold of a rope which hung from the fore-chains. In another moment he was onboard, and rushing frantically down into the cabin.

In the meantime we had been swept astern of the ship, and being quite
out of her lee, were at the mercy of the tremendous sea which was still
running. We made a determined effort to put back, but our little boat
was like a feather in the breath of the simoom. We saw at a glance that
the doom of the unfortunate artist was sealed.

As our distance from the wreck rapidly increased, the madman (for as
such only could we regard him) was seen to emerge from the companion-
way, up which, by dint of a strength that appeared superhuman, he
dragged, bodily, the oblong box. While we gazed in the extremity of
astonishment, he passed, rapidly, several turns of a three-inch rope, first
around the box and then around his body. In another instant both body
and box were in the sea — disappearing suddenly, at once and forever.

We lingered awhile, sadly upon our oars, with our eyes riveted upon the spot. At length we pulled steadily away. The silence remained unbroken for an hour, so heavy were all our hearts. Finally, I hazarded a remark.

"Did you observe, captain, how suddenly they sank? I confess that I entertained some feeble hope of his final deliverance, when I saw him lash himself to the box and commit himself to the sea."

"They sank as a matter of course," replied the captain. "They will soon rise again, however—but not till the salt melts."

"The salt!" I ejaculated.

"Hush!" said the captain, pointing to the wife and sisters of the deceased. "We must talk of these things at some more appropriate time."

We suffered much and made a narrow escape, but fortune befriended us,
as well as our mates in the longboat. We landed more dead than alive,
after four days of intense distress, upon the beach opposite Roanoke Island.
We remained here a week, and at length obtained a passage to New York.

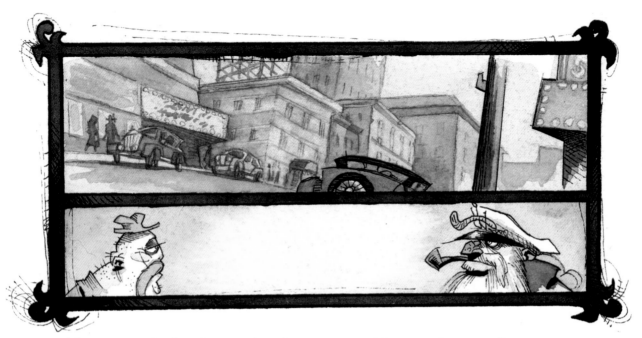

About a month after the loss of the *Independence*, I happened to meet Captain Hardy in Broadway. Our conversation turned, naturally, upon the disaster, and especially upon the sad fate of poor Wyatt. I thus learned the following particulars.

The artist had engaged passage for himself, wife, two sisters, and a servant. His wife was, indeed, as she had been represented, a most lovely and most accomplished woman.

On the morning of the fourteenth of June (the day in which I first visited the ship), the lady suddenly sickened and died. The young husband was frantic with grief — but circumstances imperatively forbade the deferring his voyage to New York.

It was necessary to take to her mother the corpse of his adored wife, and, on the other hand, the universal prejudice which would prevent his doing so openly was well known. Nine-tenths of the passengers would have abandoned the ship rather than take passage with a dead body.

In this dilemma, Captain Hardy arranged that the corpse, being first partially embalmed, and packed, with a large quantity of salt, in a box of suitable dimensions, should be conveyed onboard as merchandise.

Nothing was to be said of the lady's decease; and, as it was well understood that Mr. Wyatt had engaged passage for his wife, it became necessary that some person should personate her during the voyage. This the deceased's lady's-maid was easily prevailed on to do. The extra stateroom, originally engaged for this girl, during her mistress's life, was now merely retained. In this stateroom the pseudowife slept, of course, every night. In the daytime she performed, to the best of her ability, the part of her mistress — whose person, it had been carefully ascertained, was unknown to any of the passengers onboard.

My own mistake arose, naturally enough, through too careless, too inquisitive, and too impulsive a temperament. But of late, it is a rare thing that I sleep soundly at night. There is a countenance which haunts me, turn as I will. There is an hysterical laugh which will forever ring within my ears.

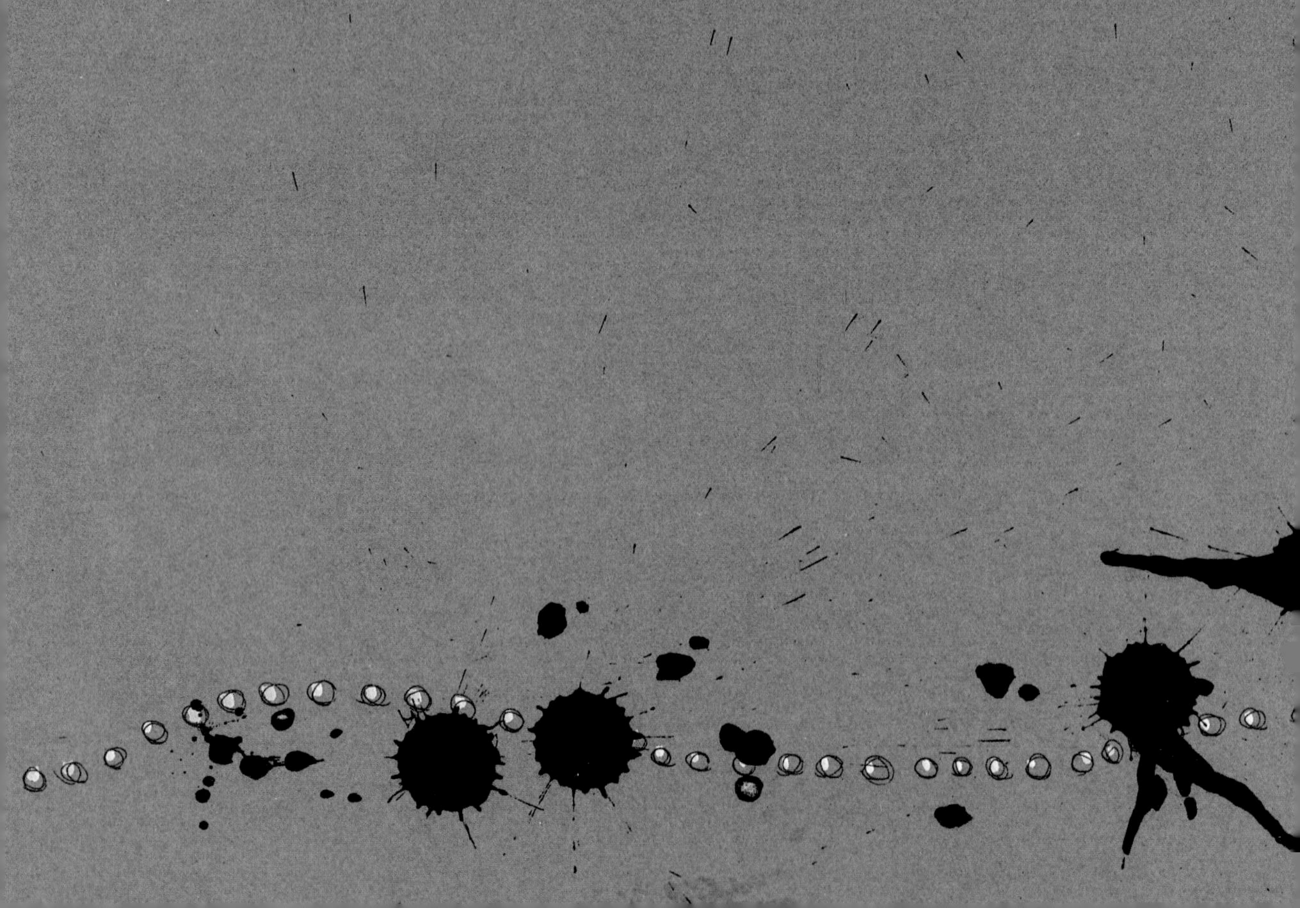

The Facts in the Case of M. Valdemar

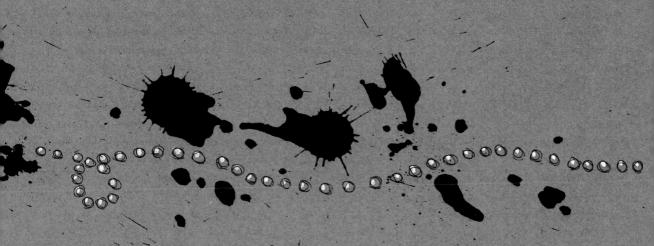

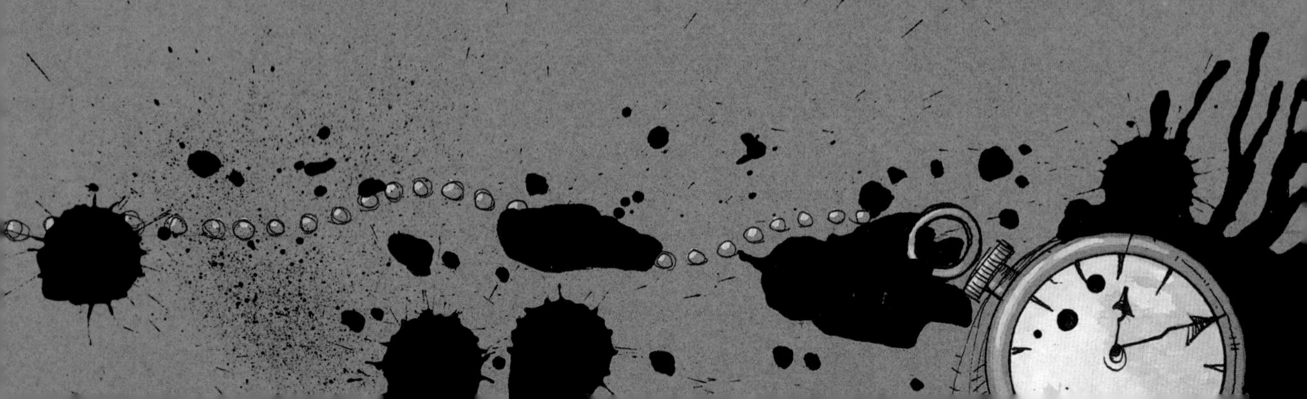

Of course I shall not pretend to consider it any matter for wonder that the extraordinary case of M. Valdemar has excited discussion. It would have been a miracle had it not — especially under the circumstances. Through the desire of all parties concerned, to keep the affair from the public until we had further opportunities for investigation — a garbled or exaggerated account made its way into society, and became the source of many unpleasant misrepresentations, and, very naturally, of a great deal of disbelief.

It is now rendered necessary that I give the facts — as far as I comprehend them myself. They are, succinctly, these:

My attention, for the last three years,
had been repeatedly drawn to the subject
of mesmerism; and, about nine months ago,
it occurred to me there had been a very remarkable
omission: no person had as yet been mesmerized *in
articulo mortis*. It remained to be seen, first, whether,
in such condition, there existed in the patient any
susceptibility to the magnetic influence; secondly,
whether, if any existed, it was impaired or increased
by the condition; thirdly, to what extent, or for how long
a period, the encroachments of death might be arrested
by the process.

fig. 92

fig. 126

In looking around me for some subject by whose means I might test these particulars, I was brought to think of my friend, M. Ernest Valdemar, the well-known compiler of the *Bibliotheca Forensica*, M. Valdemar, who has resided at Harlem, NY, since the year 1839, is (or was) particularly noticeable for the extreme spareness of his person and, also, for the whiteness of his whiskers, in violent contrast to the blackness of his hair — the latter, in consequence, being very generally mistaken for a wig. His temperament was markedly nervous, and rendered him a good subject for mesmeric experiment.

M. ERNEST VALDEMAR

fig. 84

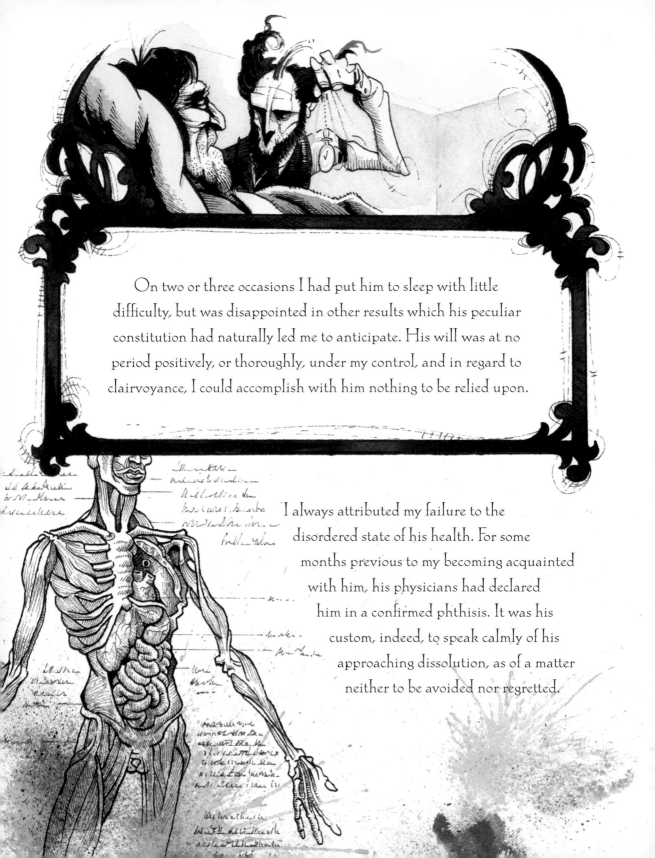

On two or three occasions I had put him to sleep with little difficulty, but was disappointed in other results which his peculiar constitution had naturally led me to anticipate. His will was at no period positively, or thoroughly, under my control, and in regard to clairvoyance, I could accomplish with him nothing to be relied upon.

I always attributed my failure to the disordered state of his health. For some months previous to my becoming acquainted with him, his physicians had declared him in a confirmed phthisis. It was his custom, indeed, to speak calmly of his approaching dissolution, as of a matter neither to be avoided nor regretted.

When the ideas to which I have alluded first occurred to me, it was very natural that I should think of M. Valdemar. I knew the steady philosophy of the man too well to apprehend any scruples from him; and he had no relatives in America who would be likely to interfere. I spoke to him frankly upon the subject, and, to my surprise, his interest seemed vividly excited. His disease was of that character which would admit of exact calculation in respect to the epoch of its termination in death; and it was finally arranged between us that he would send for me about twenty-four hours before the period announced by his physicians as that of his decease.

It is now rather more than seven months since I received from M. Valdemar himself, the subjoined note:

My dear P——,

You may as well come *now*. D—— and F—— are agreed that I cannot hold out beyond tomorrow midnight, and I think they have hit the time very nearly.

VALDEMAR

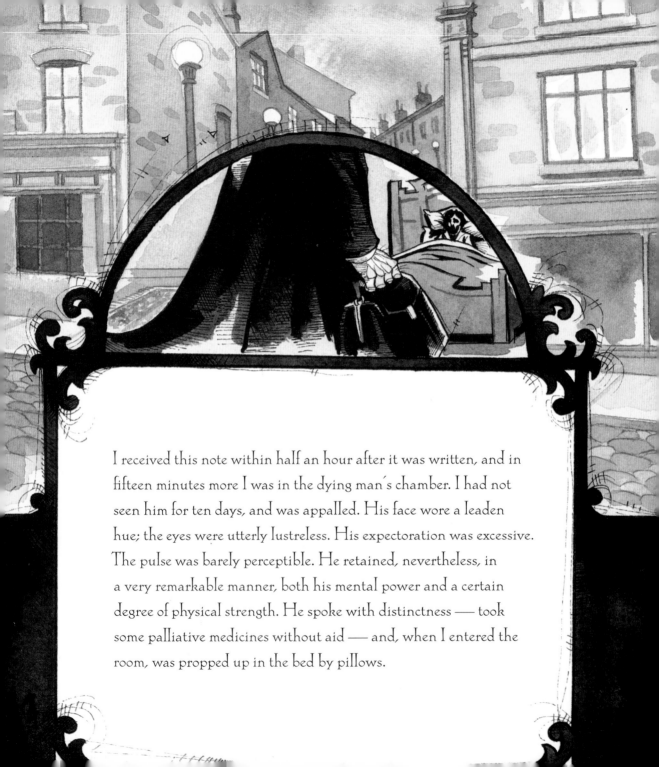

I received this note within half an hour after it was written, and in fifteen minutes more I was in the dying man's chamber. I had not seen him for ten days, and was appalled. His face wore a leaden hue; the eyes were utterly lustreless. His expectoration was excessive. The pulse was barely perceptible. He retained, nevertheless, in a very remarkable manner, both his mental power and a certain degree of physical strength. He spoke with distinctness — took some palliative medicines without aid — and, when I entered the room, was propped up in the bed by pillows.

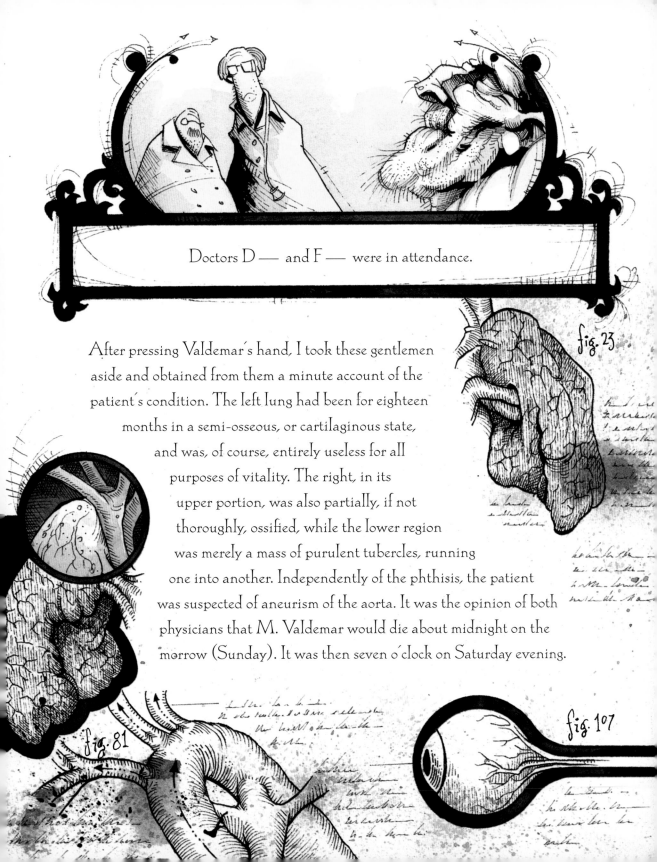

Doctors D —— and F —— were in attendance.

After pressing Valdemar's hand, I took these gentlemen aside and obtained from them a minute account of the patient's condition. The left lung had been for eighteen months in a semi-osseous, or cartilaginous state, and was, of course, entirely useless for all purposes of vitality. The right, in its upper portion, was also partially, if not thoroughly, ossified, while the lower region was merely a mass of purulent tubercles, running one into another. Independently of the phthisis, the patient was suspected of aneurism of the aorta. It was the opinion of both physicians that M. Valdemar would die about midnight on the morrow (Sunday). It was then seven o'clock on Saturday evening.

fig. 23

fig. 81

fig. 107

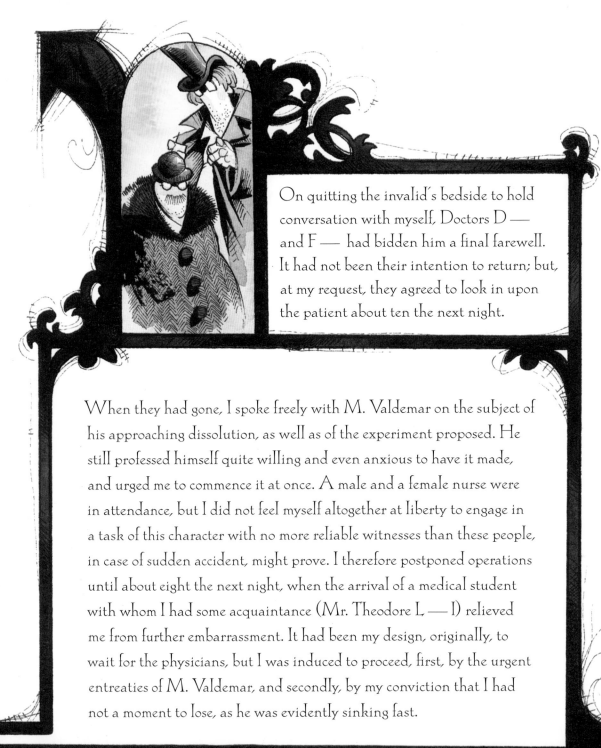

On quitting the invalid's bedside to hold conversation with myself, Doctors D—— and F—— had bidden him a final farewell. It had not been their intention to return; but, at my request, they agreed to look in upon the patient about ten the next night.

When they had gone, I spoke freely with M. Valdemar on the subject of his approaching dissolution, as well as of the experiment proposed. He still professed himself quite willing and even anxious to have it made, and urged me to commence it at once. A male and a female nurse were in attendance, but I did not feel myself altogether at liberty to engage in a task of this character with no more reliable witnesses than these people, in case of sudden accident, might prove. I therefore postponed operations until about eight the next night, when the arrival of a medical student with whom I had some acquaintance (Mr. Theodore L—— l) relieved me from further embarrassment. It had been my design, originally, to wait for the physicians, but I was induced to proceed, first, by the urgent entreaties of M. Valdemar, and secondly, by my conviction that I had not a moment to lose, as he was evidently sinking fast.

Mr. L — I was so kind as to accede to my desire that he would take notes of all that occurred, and it is from his memoranda that what I now have to relate is, for the most part, either condensed or copied verbatim.

It wanted about five minutes of eight when, taking the patient's hand, I begged him to state, as distinctly as he could, to Mr. L — I, whether he (M. Valdemar) was entirely willing that I should make the experiment of mesmerizing him in his then condition.

He replied feebly, yet quite audibly,

"Yes, I wish to be mesmerized" —

adding immediately afterward,

"I fear you have deferred it too long."

While he spoke thus, I commenced the passes which I had already found most effectual in subduing him. He was evidently influenced with the first lateral stroke of my hand across his forehead; but although I exerted all my powers, no farther perceptible effect was induced until some minutes after ten o'clock, when Doctors D —— and F —— called, according to appointment.

I explained to them what I designed, and as they opposed no objection, saying that the patient was already in the death agony, I proceeded without hesitation —— exchanging, however, the lateral passes for downward ones, and directing my gaze entirely into the right eye of the sufferer.

By this time his pulse was imperceptible and his breathing was stertorous and at intervals of half a minute.

This condition was nearly unaltered for a quarter of an hour. At the expiration of this period, however, a natural although a very deep sigh escaped the bosom of the dying man. The patient's extremities were of an icy coldness.

At five minutes before eleven I perceived unequivocal signs of the mesmeric influence. The glassy roll of the eye was exchanged for that expression of uneasy inward examination which is never seen except in cases of sleep-waking, and which it is quite impossible to mistake. With a few rapid lateral passes I made the lids quiver, as in incipient sleep, and with a few more I closed them altogether. I was not satisfied, however, with this until I had completely stiffened the limbs of the slumberer, after placing them in a seemingly easy position. The legs were at full length; the arms were nearly so, and reposed on the bed at a moderate distance from the loins.

The head was very slightly elevated.

When I had accomplished this, it was fully midnight, and I requested the gentlemen present to examine M. Valdemar's condition. After a few experiments, they admitted him to be in an unusually perfect state of mesmeric trance. The curiosity of both the physicians was greatly excited.

We left M. Valdemar entirely undisturbed until about three o'clock in the morning, when I approached him and found him in precisely the same condition — that is to say, he lay in the same position; the pulse was imperceptible; the breathing was gentle (scarcely noticeable, unless through the application of a mirror to the lips); the eyes were closed naturally; and the limbs were as rigid and as cold as marble. Still, the general appearance was certainly not that of death.

I determined to hazard a few words of conversation.

"M. Valdemar," I said, "are you asleep?"

He made no answer, but I perceived a tremor about the lips, and was thus induced to repeat the question, again and again. At its third repetition, his whole frame was agitated by a very slight shivering; the eyelids unclosed themselves so far as to display a white line of the ball; the lips moved sluggishly, and from between them, in a barely audible whisper, issued the words:

"Yes; asleep now. Do not wake me! Let me die so!"

I here felt the limbs and found them as rigid as ever. The right arm, as before, obeyed the direction of my hand. I questioned the sleep-waker again:

"Do you still feel pain in the breast, M. Valdemar?"

The answer now was immediate, but even less audible than before:

"No pain — I am dying."

Dr. F expressed unbounded astonishment. After feeling the pulse and applying a mirror to the lips, he requested me to speak to the sleep-waker again. I did so, saying:

"M. Valdemar, do you still sleep?"

As before, some minutes elapsed ere a reply was made; and during the interval the dying man seemed to be collecting his energies to speak. At my fourth repetition of the question, he said, very faintly, almost inaudibly:

"Yes; still asleep — dying."

It was now the opinion, or rather the wish, of the physicians, that M. Valdemar should be suffered to remain undisturbed in his present apparently tranquil condition, until death should supervene — and this, it was generally agreed, must now take place within a few minutes. I concluded, however, to speak to him once more, and merely repeated my previous question.

While I spoke, there came a marked change over the countenance of the sleep-waker. The eyes rolled themselves slowly open, the pupils disappearing upwardly; the skin generally assumed a cadaverous hue, resembling not so much parchment as white paper; and the circular hectic spots which, hitherto, had been strongly defined in the center of each cheek, went out at once. I use this expression because the suddenness of their departure put me in mind of nothing so much as the extinguishment of a candle by a puff of the breath. The upper lip, at the same time, writhed itself away from the teeth, which it had previously covered completely, while the lower jaw fell with an audible jerk, leaving the mouth widely extended, and disclosing in full view the swollen and blackened tongue.

I presume that no member of the party then present had been unaccustomed to deathbed horrors, but so hideous beyond conception was the appearance of M. Valdemar at this moment that there was a general shrinking back from the region of the bed.

I now feel that I have reached a point of this narrative at which every reader will be startled into positive disbelief. It is my business, however, simply to proceed.

There was no longer the faintest sign of vitality in M. Valdemar; and concluding him to be dead, we were consigning him to the charge of the nurses, when a strong vibratory motion was observable in the tongue. This continued for perhaps a minute. At the expiration of this period, there issued from the distended and motionless jaws a voice — such as it would be madness in me to attempt describing, for the simple reason that no similar sounds have ever jarred upon the ear of humanity. The voice seemed to reach our ears — at least mine — from a vast distance, or from some deep cavern within the earth.

M. Valdemar spoke — obviously in reply to the question I had propounded to him a few minutes before. I had asked him, it will be remembered, if he still slept. He now said:

"Yes; —no; —I have been sleeping—and now—now—I am dead."

No person present even affected to deny the unutterable, shuddering horror which these few words, thus uttered, were so well calculated to convey.

Mr. L — I (the student) swooned.

The nurses immediately left the chamber, and could not be induced to return.

My own impressions I would not pretend to render intelligible to the reader. For nearly an hour we busied ourselves, in endeavors to revive Mr. L — I. When he came to himself, we addressed ourselves again to an investigation of M. Valdemar's condition.

It remained in all respects as I have last described it, with the exception that the mirror no longer afforded evidence of respiration. An attempt to draw blood from the arm failed.

The only real indication, indeed, of the mesmeric influence, was now found in the vibratory movement of the tongue, whenever I addressed M. Valdemar a question. He seemed to be making an effort to reply, but had no longer sufficient volition. To queries put to him by any other person than myself he seemed utterly insensible — although I endeavored to place each member of the company in mesmeric rapport with him. Other nurses were procured; and at ten o'clock I left the house in company with the two physicians and Mr. L — l.

In the afternoon we all called again to see the patient. His condition remained precisely the same. We had now some discussion as to the propriety and feasibility of awakening him; but we had little difficulty in agreeing that no good purpose would be served by so doing. It was evident that, so far, death (or what is usually termed death) had been arrested by the mesmeric process. It seemed clear to us all that to awaken M. Valdemar would be merely to insure his instant, or at least his speedy, dissolution.

From this period until the close of last week — *an interval of nearly seven months* — we continued to make daily calls at M. Valdemar's house, accompanied, now and then, by medical and other friends. All this time the sleeper-waker remained *exactly* as I have last described him. The nurses' attentions were continual.

It was on Friday last that we finally resolved to make the experiment of awakening, or attempting to awaken him; and it is the (perhaps) unfortunate result of this latter experiment which has given rise to so much discussion in private circles — to so much of what I cannot help thinking unwarranted popular feeling.

For the purpose of relieving M. Valdemar from the mesmeric trance, I made use of the customary passes. These, for a time, were unsuccessful. The first indication of revival was afforded by a partial descent of the iris. It was observed, as especially remarkable, that this lowering of the pupil was accompanied by the profuse outflowing of a yellowish ichor (from beneath the lids) of a pungent and highly offensive odor.

Dr. F —— then intimated a desire to have me put a question. I did so, as follows:

"M. Valdemar, can you explain to us what are your feelings or wishes now?"

The tongue quivered, or rather rolled violently in the mouth (although the jaws and lips remained rigid as before), and at length the same hideous voice which I have already described broke forth:

"For God's sake! — quick! — quick! — put me to sleep — or, quick! — waken me! — quick! — I say to you that I am dead!"

I was thoroughly unnerved, and for an instant remained undecided what to do.

At first I made an endeavor to recompose the patient; but, failing in this through total abeyance of the will, I retraced my steps and as earnestly struggled to awaken him. In this attempt I soon saw that I should be successful — or at least I soon fancied that my success would be complete — and I am sure that all in the room were prepared to see the patient awaken.

For what really occurred, however, it is quite impossible that any human being could have been prepared.

As I rapidly made the mesmeric passes, amid ejaculations of

"DEAD! DEAD!"

absolutely bursting from the tongue and not from the lips of the sufferer, his whole frame at once — within the space of a single minute, or even less — shrunk — crumbled — absolutely rotted away beneath my hands.

Upon the bed, before that whole
company, there lay a nearly liquid mass of
loathsome — of detestable putridity.